Live From The Fifth Grade

Other books by
Colleen O'Shaughnessy McKenna

Too Many Murphys

Fourth Grade Is a Jinx

Fifth Grade: Here Comes Trouble

Eenie, Meanie, Murphy, No!

Murphy's Island

Merry Christmas, Miss McConnell!

The Truth About Sixth Grade

Mother Murphy

The Brightest Light

Camp Murphy

Cousins: Not Quite Sisters

Cousins: Stuck in the Middle

Good Grief . . . Third Grade

LIVE FROM THE FIFTH GRADE

COLLEEN O'SHAUGHNESSY McKENNA

SCHOLASTIC
HARDCOVER

Scholastic Inc.
New York

Library of Congress Cataloging-in-Publication Data

McKenna, Colleen O'Shaughnessy.
    Live from the fifth grade / Colleen O'Shaughnessy McKenna.
        p.   cm.
    Summary: Roger Friday loves to play tricks on Marsha Cessano, but when he investigates a robbery at school, he finds the best man for the job is Marsha.

ISBN 0-590-46684-4

    [1. Practical jokes — Fiction.   2. Stealing — Fiction.   3. Schools — Fiction.]   I. Title.
PZ7.M478675Li   1994
[Fic] — dc20   93-13706
                                                                       CIP
                                                                       AC

12 11 10 9 8 7 6 5 4 3 2 1   4 5 6 7 8 9/9
                                                                       37

Printed in the U.S.A.

First printing, September 1994

*Dedicated with love and best wishes
to a truly funny and kind man — Roger Friday.
Special thanks to his creators,
Dr. and Mrs. J. R. Friday,
his better half, Kathy,
and his four terrific children:
J. R., Elizabeth, Meredith, and Matt.*

Live From The Fifth Grade

Chapter One

The trouble all started when I brought a dead snake to school. I'd first seen it on my way to the bus stop, but walked past it, thinking it was a garden hose. Then I noticed its little face. The tongue was sticking out, as if it had tried to scream at the last minute. It looked pretty good. Even better, only a few parts were stuck to the road. The rest of it was all dried flat. This snake was definitely too good to pass up, so I emptied out my Sacred Heart gym bag and gently put in the snake. I smiled, knowing *exactly* what I was going to do with it.

The school bus was already turning on to Heberton Avenue, so I started to run. As soon as

I climbed into the bus, I let Patrick Frank, my best friend, peek inside the bag.

"Whoa, cool snake," said Patrick. "Are you going to stuff it and keep it in your room?"

I shook my head. "No, my mom felt sick when she saw my rabbit's foot! Besides, Patrick, this snake has a job, a mission."

Patrick grinned and leaned closer. "What's that?"

"I thought I'd surprise Marsha with it."

Patrick howled. He laughed so loud a seventh-grader whipped around and told him to clam up. Patrick turned bright red and slunk down in his seat. He doesn't like to get anyone taller than him mad. But when I picked up the snake by its head and pretended it was a snake-phone, Patrick laughed again.

"Hello, operator . . . I'd like to make a person-to-snake call, please . . ."

Patrick snorted.

"Reverse the charges . . ." I twirled the end of the snake around my finger like a phone cord.

"Ohhh, look at Roger!" A little girl giggled behind me.

The seventh-grader stood up and turned around

again. But when he saw my snake, he grinned and swatted me on the head with his notebook. Then he gave me a thumbs-up sign.

Truly funny people, like myself, know that the *thumbs-up sign* means the audience wants more.

"Any requests from the audience?" I asked, loosening my tie and tossing the snake back and forth in my hands.

"Yeah," called out Marsha Cessano. "I have a great request for you, Roger. Go jump in a lake."

Of course I ignored her. Marsha is the biggest pest in the fifth grade.

Next I hung the snake on top of my head with the ends dangling like skinny braids. I crossed my eyes. Some of the kids started to clap. That's when the bus driver started glaring into the rearview mirror. The snake went back into my gym bag fast! I didn't want the bus driver to grab it before I could scare Marsha.

It wouldn't be the first time I used a snake to scare her, either. My first snake delivery was made way back in the first grade. That was four years ago. Marsha was way overdue for another snake surprise.

It isn't that I hate this Marsha character. It's

just that we have been trying to drive each other crazy since kindergarten and I want to keep a healthy lead. Last week she put a couple of raw eggs inside my desk and when I tossed my books inside, the eggs, and Marsha, "cracked up." Even Mrs. Pompalini smiled before she remembered she was the teacher.

It was then, while watching Marsha pick egg-shell off my science book, that I started to plan my revenge. It wasn't going to be anything stupid, like putting a tack on her chair. First-graders could think of that stuff. No. My revenge was going to be something only a mastermind like myself could arrange. It took seven days before the snake fell into my lap.

"So what's the plan, Roger?" asked Patrick as the bus pulled up in front of Sacred Heart Elementary. "This is going to be great. Marsha is going to have a spaz attack."

"I haven't got it all worked out yet, Patrick." I patted the snake before I zipped up the gym bag. Patrick and I got off the bus and walked into school. A lot of kids were gathered around the principal's office. It was the first Monday of November

4

and Sister Mary Elizabeth was collecting canned goods for the poor. She was up to her elbows in lima beans and chicken soup, way too busy to spot a fifth-grader smuggling in a dead snake.

"Should I roll up the snake like a doughnut and stick it in her lunch bag?"

Patrick shook his head. "Marsha always keeps her lunch in her backpack. Too risky, Roger."

"You're right." I continued, "Should I use the direct approach and stick it down the back of her jumper? Mrs. Pompalini is always telling her to sit up straighter."

"I dare you," said Patrick.

"Never dare a funny guy. It's dangerous."

"You are soooooo funny!"

"Thank you," I said humbly. Actually, I *am* funny. I was born that way. I don't mean funny like I have ears that stick out or a pointed nose, but I think funny. Having a sense of humor can be a gift or a curse. It's a gift if you're doing comedy acts on cable. Comedians get paid lots of money for being funny. Having a sense of humor is a *curse* if you're just a kid in the fifth grade. Nobody gives me money. Nobody claps. Teachers yell at me. Then they send me down to Sister Mary Elizabeth. When Sister finishes, she calls my parents. They yell at me, too.

In my long career at Sacred Heart Elementary, I have spent as much time in the office as the secretary, Miss Merkle. She's always nice. Secretaries see a lot of troublemakers in their job. They can spot kids who don't mean to get in trouble. Like me.

Now Marsha Cessano is another story. Not one drop of her is funny. And she's got a temper you would not believe. Did you ever watch "Popeye"? Well, picture Brutus with a ponytail, wearing a jumper. That's Marsha.

"Putting the snake down her back is a little dangerous, Rog," said Patrick. He already looked worried. "Too many witnesses. What would you say if you got caught?" He was right. No wonder he's the smartest kid in the fifth grade.

"I guess we can't have too many witnesses." I chewed on my lip for a second. "I better just stick it in her locker." I grinned, picturing Marsha's perfectly neat locker.

Patrick didn't, he frowned. "But what will you say if Sister catches you?"

6

I shrugged. "I'll just tell her that I got my locker and Marsha's mixed up." As I stuck my books in my locker, I wondered if Sister would buy that. Probably not. My locker is on the other side of the hall. Sister Mary Elizabeth doesn't believe too many of my stories. Neither do my parents. That's because none of them have a sense of humor.

If I could ever talk to God, face-to-face, I would tell him *not* to give a kid a great sense of humor . . . like mine . . . unless at least *one* parent has one, too. It's like giving a baby kangaroo to a pair of polar bears. It's not a good match. The bears are going to spend their whole life telling their kangaroo kid not to jump in the house.

As soon as the first bell rang, Marsha raced into homeroom. She always wants to be in her seat, pretending to be perfect, as soon as possible. Patrick and I got five or six drinks of water, waiting for the rest of the kids to clear the hall. When only the Binkley twins were left, I opened Marsha's locker. I gently pulled out the snake and hung it carefully around her hot pink jacket. I made sure the snake's head, with its bent, dangling tongue, was propped up against the collar so it looked ready to say, "hello."

"Great," whispered Patrick. His ears and cheeks were bright red. Patrick wasn't used to getting in trouble.

"Thanks," I whispered back. I tried not to laugh out loud. In exactly one hour the whole class would march out here to get their gym shorts and shoes.

That's when the fun would begin.

Chapter Two

Marsha was not pleased with the snake. As soon as she reached in her locker for her jacket and pulled out a snake instead, she let loose with sounds I've only heard at the zoo. By the second screech every homeroom door on the first floor flew open. Teachers ran out, kindergarten kids dropped their snacks, and one second-grader burst into tears.

It was touching to see everyone getting so involved.

"It bit me!" shrieked Marsha, tossing the snake high into the air. More shrieks as the snake bounced off her shoulder and slid across the floor. "I'm going to die." She slumped against the lockers briefly before sliding down to the floor.

I bit my lip so I wouldn't laugh. Patrick was white as a ghost.

"What in the world?" Mrs. Pompalini lunged at the snake with her yardstick.

"The snake is dead, Mrs. Pompalini," announced Patrick.

Mrs. Pompalini poked at the snake with the yardstick, then hopped to the side as if she expected an attack. "Stand back, children!"

More teachers hurried over. The music teacher splashed her coffee on the snake.

"Stop that, Helen," shouted Mrs. Pompalini. "Caffeine will just wake him up!"

The snake looked deader than ever, even bored.

"Looks pretty harmless to me," I said.

"Harmless?" screamed Marsha. In less than two seconds she had scrambled to her feet and was jabbing me in the chest. "How harmless is a poison snake? How harmless is a snake trained by a peabrain like you to attack me?"

"Hey, settle down."

Mrs. Pompalini pulled Marsha off me. "How in the world did that snake get in your locker, Marsha?"

Marsha shrugged. "I certainly didn't *invite* him!"

"Good line, Marsha."

Marsha spun around and grabbed me by the arm. "Be quiet, you . . . you monster!"

"Marsha!" Ms. Pompalini tapped her foot. "How did the snake get in your locker?"

Marsha stared down at the snake for a few minutes, as if waiting for it to give its side of the story. After a moment of silence, her head jerked up, her eyes narrowed, and she pointed to me. "Here's the criminal, Mrs. Pompalini. Creepy old Roger Friday put the snake in my locker!"

"Me?" I managed to squeak out.

"You know you did it!" shouted Marsha. "Wait till my mother hears about this. I think I'm allergic to snakes and . . ."

"Quiet!"

Chills raced down my spine. Out of the corner of my eye I watched as Sister Mary Elizabeth marched down the hall, her rosary beads swinging. Sister did not look too happy. In fact, she was wearing the look she usually saves for moments when someone sets off the fire alarm.

Even the teachers scattered.

"I want an explanation," demanded Sister. For some reason she looked straight at me.

"Roger did it," Marsha added. "I know he did."

"Don't accuse too hastily, Marsha," Mrs. Pompalini said quickly. She gave me a kind smile and suddenly I felt kind of crummy. Not crummy for scaring Marsha. That had been fun, downright enjoyable. One more shriek and her head would have shot off and rolled down the hall like a bowling ball.

But I didn't want to get Mrs. Pompalini in trouble. Maybe Sister would fire her for not being able to control her students.

"What do you have to say about all this, Mr. Friday?" asked Sister.

"Well, let me see here," I said slowly, scratching my head and kneeling down to get a better look. "Yeah, yeah, come to think of it, this snake does look familiar. In fact, this snake may be the very snake I put in my gym bag this morning!"

"I knew it!" screamed Marsha. "I want to press charges, Sister. My cousin is a lawyer — he can sue people."

"Settle down, Marsha," snapped Sister.

The next thing I knew, Sister Mary Elizabeth's

index finger was drilling into my spine as we headed down to her office. I was confused and disappointed. Why didn't I get more laughs with the snake? There had been more screaming than laughing. That was not a good sign. I'd have to rethink the whole set-up. I could deal with getting into trouble, or even getting kicked out of fifth grade. But, what a waste of a perfectly good snake.

Chapter Three

Sister and I marched right past Miss Merkle. From her sad smile I could tell she wanted to wish me luck, but there was something about Sister's finger in my back that let us all know that now was not a good time. Once the inner office door closed, Sister removed her finger and pointed to a chair.

"Sit down, Roger."

I sat, folded my hands in my lap, and tried to look baffled.

"Roger?" Sister Mary Elizabeth sank into her chair, rubbing her forehead. "Are you ready to tell me about the snake?"

"Sure, Sister!" I sat up straighter in my chair.

"There has been a huge, terrible, enormous misunderstanding."

Sister closed her eyes for a long moment. When she opened them she frowned, as if she hoped I'd disappeared. "Go on, Roger."

"Okay, let me see." I cleared my throat. Maybe an explanation would come to me. "You see, I found this snake on my way to the bus stop. It was lying in the middle of the road. Since all the snake's blood and guts had dried up already, it was easy to lift up from the road."

Sister shuddered. She glanced at the white phone on her desk. Her fingers were moving up and down. She could hardly wait to call my mother and let her know I was in trouble again.

"You should have left the snake on the road, Roger. Why on earth did you sneak it into school to terrorize a classmate? Poor Marsha screamed so loudly I heard her all the way down the hall."

"We're lucky her shrieks didn't break every window in the school, Sister," I said.

"That's not funny, Roger." She started rubbing her forehead again.

"Maybe you should go back to the convent and lie down, Sister."

Sister put her face in her hands. From behind her fingers, I heard, "You have exactly *one* minute to stop trying to be a comedian, and tell me exactly why you put the snake in Marsha's locker." She looked up and checked her watch. "One minute before I pick up that phone and call your mother."

Why do adults always want to drag mothers into sticky situations? It's not as if I get in trouble just to make my mom miserable. She would feel terrible when she got the call. I like my mom a lot. She's cool, and she's always in a good mood.

"What's it going to be, Roger?" Sister paused for two seconds and reached for the phone. Of course I started talking a mile a minute as if the F.B.I. were on its way over. "Well, Sister, I guess the *real* reason I felt I had to bring the snake to school was . . ." I stopped and prayed an explanation would come to me, hoping guardian angels were real and that mine had a sense of humor.

"You see, as soon as I saw this snake all squashed on the road, I felt kind of bad leaving him . . . I mean, there was no medical help in sight. Sacred Heart has taught me that even the lowest snake is . . . is still one of God's little creatures."

16

Sister Mary Elizabeth's left eyebrow went up. It didn't come down.

"Snakes do not have a soul, Roger."

"But Sister, do we know that for sure? I mean, Noah did take two of them on the ark. Besides, my bus was coming and I had to act fast. For all I knew, the snake could have been in some sort of coma."

Sister sighed and held up her hand to stop me. "Sacred Heart is an elementary school, Roger, not an emergency room for snakes. Now, for the last time, Mr. Friday, I want you to tell me why you put the snake in Marsha's locker instead of leaving it on the side of the road where it belonged." Sister crossed her arms and leaned forward. "You knew it was dead."

My last card was about to be played. "You're right, Sister. I knew the snake was dead." I drew in a deep breath, blinked about ten times, and tried to look sincere. "I . . . I wanted to bring it to *you*, Sister. So you could bless it and we could have a short prayer and bury it out behind the cafeteria and — "

I never got a chance to finish. Sister was already on the phone. "Your son, Roger, is in trouble, *again,* Mrs. Friday." Sister's voice grew stronger with each word. "He terrorized a poor little girl with a snake."

Sister was quiet for a moment. "Yes . . . yes, the snake *was* dead when he found it." Sister started nodding her head over and over again to whatever my mother was saying. My heart started to beat with hope. Maybe my mom was defending me, telling Sister that she was downright proud that her son cared about one of God's little creatures. I *did* care about that dead snake. With any luck it might be the last specimen of a rare and special species. More and more people would hear about me. I could end up a hero.

"I'm glad you agree with me, Mrs. Friday," Sister said quickly. "Detention will certainly be a step in the right direction."

What? Detention?

"I totally agree," replied Sister. "Roger can start detention right after school today. You can pick him up at five by the office entrance."

As Sister Mary Elizabeth hung up the telephone and turned to face me, she drew in a deep breath as if she had just climbed a very tall and difficult mountain. "Your mother is *very* upset, Roger . . ."

I knew I was in trouble. I watched Sister's mouth move faster and faster.

The bottom line was this: Sister Mary Elizabeth thought if I stayed after school for the next nine trillion weeks, so I could think about my actions, I would be a better kid. I would get into heaven faster, and Marsha's parents wouldn't want to throw me in jail. The whole world was going to be a better place once I scraped three thousand wads of old gum from underneath the bleachers of the Sacred Heart gym.

No one ever said being funny was easy.

Chapter Four

Sister walked me back to homeroom, probably to make sure I wouldn't make a run for it. Actually, I'm pretty cool about getting in trouble. Some jokes get a laugh and some jokes get me detention. I can live with it. At least Patrick didn't get caught. His parents might have thought of me as a bad influence. *That* would not be funny.

My class was getting ready to change classes for reading. As soon as I walked in the door, I saw "trouble" staring at me. Marsha stuck out her tongue and was happy to hear I had to stay after school forever.

"I hope they lock you in the furnace room and throw away the key," she barked. She squinted up her eyes and shot me a look that was probably supposed to zap me into a black hole.

Patrick apologized. "I should have tried to talk you out of it, Roger. Both of us are to blame."

I just grinned. "No hard feelings."

Marsha's cheeks blazed red. It drives her crazy when I refuse to get mad.

I kept my cool all day. As soon as the buses were called, I went down to the little room next to the cafeteria to let Mr. Doyle, the janitor, know I was ready for duty.

"Come on in, Roger." Mr. Doyle always speaks slowly, carefully. He poured me a little cup of hot chocolate from his silver thermos and handed me a putty knife. "I sure can use the help, Roger." Mr. Doyle pointed to a hook on the wall where I could hang up my tie and sweater. He loaned me an old sweatshirt from the lost and found so I wouldn't get dirty. After that, the two of us went upstairs.

I like spending time with Mr. Doyle. My mother says that he doesn't have ". . . a mean bone in his body." Mr. Doyle looks the same age as my dad, but when he was a little kid he got hit by a truck. After the accident, his brain didn't work as well.

But his brain works well enough to keep Sacred Heart looking great. Even the eighth-graders yell at anyone who even thinks about spray painting a wall or stuffing gym socks down a toilet. The whole school knows how much Sacred Heart means to Mr. Doyle.

After I helped Mr. Doyle sweep up some classrooms, we went into the gym. Berry-the-Strawberry, the greatest hooper in Sacred Heart's history, and five other eighth-graders from our school, were warming up before the kids from the public schools came over to practice for the big city tournament. Berry was already over six feet tall and could dunk as well as some of the kids from the high school. Who said detention was no fun? I could watch him and learn a few things for my own game.

"Those boys sure can play good, right, Rog?"

"They sure can, especially Berry." I tossed a wad of purple gum into the metal can. Twank! Perfect shot.

"Maybe one day you can play with those guys," said Mr. Doyle. "Okay, Roger?"

I just nodded, twanking another wad into the

trash can. I would *never* be good enough to play with Strawberry and his friends.

"Hot dog! Work as a team!"

I turned. A skinny guy was leaning against the wall. He was shaking his head as if Berry and the other starters weren't a bit cool. I had seen him before — he went to Sacred Heart last year and then transferred to public school. His name was Jimmy Rattner, but everyone called him Gym Rat. He never played any sports, he just hung around and made fun of the kids who did.

I helped Mr. Doyle until five, then ran outside and got into my dad's car. As soon as I buckled up my seatbelt, I knew it was going to be a long drive. My father was staring straight ahead, his knuckles bulging out of his clenched hands as he gripped the steering wheel.

"Your mother called me at the office," he said quietly. "I'm very, very disappointed."

"If funny bones came with a guarantee, I'd send mine back," I offered.

My father didn't smile. He just yelled at me for the next twenty blocks till we pulled in to our driveway.

Once we got in the house, both of my parents took turns yelling at me.

"You're not just disgracing yourself, Roger," my father informed me. "You are bringing shame to the whole family."

That's when my mother started to cry. She buried her face in my dog's fur. "And to think you're an altar boy," she wailed behind Leaks's flea collar.

"It was supposed to be a joke," I said. I promised my parents that the next time Sister Mary Elizabeth called them, it would be to congratulate them on having such a nice son.

My mother looked up from the dog. My dad set his ginger ale down with a thump. Nobody smiled. Nobody looked as if they believed one word.

By the time I got on the bus the next morning, I felt terrible.

"What's wrong with you, Roger?" asked Patrick.

"I practically signed an oath in blood to my parents that I would sit at my desk and be perfect for the rest of the year," I explained. "I'll probably be the most boring person in America by the end of the week."

"I guess your parents were mad about the snake."

"Marsha is ruining my life." I knew I could trust

Patrick. He is very, very smart. He gets embarrassed when teachers make a big deal over his brain. "It's a gift from God," Sister Mary Elizabeth always says, then she makes the Sign of the Cross and pats him on the head. On holy days, Sister always asks Patrick to wear a suit and read the prayers at Mass. Patrick says he wishes he wasn't so smart, but he can't help it. Just like I can't help having a sense of humor. But Sister Mary Elizabeth doesn't think my sense of humor is a gift from God. The only time she makes the Sign of the Cross about me is after she rolls her eyes and whispers, "Lord, give me strength."

"That was a cool snake," Patrick said softly. "His left eye was closed, like he was winking at us."

I nodded. That was a nice snake all right. He had probably been a funny snake.

As soon as Patrick and I got off the bus and went inside the classroom, we heard Marsha laughing. "My mom's newest television for the kitchen is only five inches wide. It's so cute." Marsha spends a lot of her time bragging about how rich she is. "My house has fourteen rooms. We've got a car phone. We have three color televisions. . . ."

Being born funny can be tough. But sometimes I think being born rich is even worse.

As I sat down in my seat, I smiled at Mrs. Pompalini. She seemed sorry she had screamed yesterday. With five boys of her own, she must have realized that a dead snake wasn't worth yelling about. She had probably screamed because Marsha was running around in circles like her hair was on fire.

"Good morning, Mrs. Pompalini." I wanted her to know I didn't hold a grudge.

"Good morning, Roger." Mrs. Pompalini put her hands on her hips and grinned. "Is there anything in your bookbag I should know about?"

"Two dead skunks." We both laughed.

The rest of the day went pretty quickly. Marsha kept looking at me as if I had some evil plan in mind. I didn't. It took all of my concentration to keep my sense of humor in. Like when Marsha raised her hand and asked if she could go to the restroom, I had to bite my tongue to keep from saying, "Sorry, Marsha. We only have restrooms for humans."

But since I wasn't allowed to use my sense of humor, I just stared at my math ditto. Even when

Marsha marched past my desk and knocked my pencil on the floor, I didn't look up. The old Rog would have bent down and tried to trip her, but the new, boring, no-sense-of-humor-allowed Roger just reached in his desk for a new pencil. It was pitiful.

I had promised my parents to lay low for the rest of the semester. But I had been smart enough not to promise the whole year. In January I had plans to get even with Marsha. So every time Marsha shut my book, or slammed my locker, or made me look bad in class, I put a little mark on my wooden ruler. A notch for every crummy thing she did to me.

I was hoping she wouldn't get a chance to fill up the whole ruler. I would be beyond repair by then.

I watched as Marsha left the room. I had promised my parents I would lie low until January first. But come January second, I would rise again. Come January second, Marsha Cessano would be screaming nonstop.

Chapter Five

During lunch, Marsha found a black spider in her lunch bag. She discovered it was rubber when she tossed it across the room where it bounced off an eighth-grader.

Of course everyone looked at me. A few kids even pounded me on the back. "Great spider!" they said. But I couldn't take credit for the joke. The new, boring, perfect Roger couldn't have put the spider in Marsha's lunch bag. Patrick had. He was sitting next to me, red-faced and shredding his napkin to tiny bits. It was the first time Patrick had *ever* done anything like that. I laughed extra hard. Since Patrick was new to practical jokes, I had to encourage him. I think, in his own way, he was trying to be loyal to me. Kind of like picking up the baton.

"You put the spider in my lunch bag!" shouted Marsha. She marched down the aisle and stuck her face in mine. She was so close I could see the tiny hairs in her nose. "I'm going to call my cousin and *sue* you, mister!"

I started to laugh. I could just picture Marsha and me standing before a judge with a rubber spider marked exhibit A.

"Marsha, wait!" I took a few steps after her. Patrick's eyes were ready to pop out and roll down the table. He probably thought I was going to turn him in. "I have something to tell you."

Marsha made a neat pivot and crossed her arms, waiting. "I just hope for your sake that it's an apology, 'cause I was on my way to Sister's office right now."

I tried to look sincere. "Well, not really. I just wanted to say that you really shouldn't have thrown the spider away, Marsha. He looked like a relative of yours."

I guess I hit a nerve because Marsha started screaming that she wanted to get me out of her life and blah, blah, blah, with the whole cafeteria watching. From the eighth-grade section, Strawberry and one of his friends started to clap and whistle.

The next thing I knew, Mrs. Pompalini was hurrying down the aisle, "What in the world is going on now?"

"Roger Friday put a hairy spider in my lunch bag!" shouted Marsha. She leaned over and shook my arm. "Why don't you just leave me alone, Roger?"

Mrs. Pompalini tried to pry Marsha off me. Marsha was working herself into a major spaz attack. Her whole face was red and she kept poking me. Lots of kids were laughing. I tried to look over at Patrick to see if he was enjoying himself. Then I noticed Marsha's face. She was getting ready either to explode or cry. She was chewing on her lip and yanking down hard on her bangs. That's the signal she's about to lose it.

Mrs. Pompalini held both of Marsha's hands in hers. "Now calm down and tell me what is going on."

Marsha covered her face and started to cry. "He put a tarantula in my lunch. Why does he keep scaring me?"

30

When I saw the tears rolling down her cheeks, I felt bad. Why did Marsha have to go and start crying? The snake had been dead and the spider was fake. She didn't have to wrestle them or anything.

Sarah and Collette, Marsha's two best friends, stood up and filled Mrs. Pompalini in on all the facts.

"Marsha reached in to grab her sandwich and the spider jumped right onto her hand," reported Sarah.

"It was a rubber spider," I added quickly. "Rubber can't bite."

Mrs. Pompalini glared at me. "Honestly, Roger. First the dead snake and now a spider. Why on earth do you do these things?"

"Hey, who said I did?" I tried to look completely innocent. "Why am I always the first one blamed?"

Marsha looked up, wiping each eye with the sleeve of her sweater. "You *know* you did it, Roger. Nobody else has your mean peabrain to think up something this . . . this disgusting."

Kids started to laugh and Mrs. Pompalini clapped her hands. "Children, go outside as soon as you finish your lunch." She waited till the other kids sat back down, and then put her hand on my shoulder. "Roger, I am not accusing you. I know we do not have any *proof* that you put the spider in Marsha's lunch bag. But you *did* put the snake in her locker, and the two crimes are rather similar."

"Call the police," suggested Marsha. "Have them dust the spider for Roger's crummy finger-prints. . . ."

I smiled, wondering if Marsha was serious. How could you dust eight little rubber legs?

"I can handle this, Marsha," said Mrs. Pompalini. "Roger, I am asking for your cooper-ation." Mrs. Pompalini put her arm around Marsha's shoulder. Marsha tried to muster up an-other tear, but she was dry. She coughed weakly instead. "Now, for the last time . . . *did* you put the spider in Marsha's lunch, Roger?"

I was about to say, "Of course not. And frankly, members of the court, I am a little insulted that . . . ." But I couldn't. I didn't want to go on. Be-cause then I would have to tell them that Patrick had done the deed. And this was the first time Patrick had ever tried to be funny. If he got in trouble for this, he would never try again. The world might be losing a potentially funny guy.

"And if you didn't, do you know who *did* put the spider in Marsha's lunch?" Mrs. Pompalini tapped her foot as she waited for my answer.

I didn't know what to do. Anything I said was going to be wrong for somebody. The trouble is, I can't lie. I never could. Maybe it's because my mom is always saying that the truth, no matter how bad, is better than a terrific lie. "I plead the Fifth Amendment, Mrs. Pompalini. I can't answer that question." I shoved my hands in my pockets and waited for the axe to fall.

"Well, Roger. . . ." Mrs. Pompalini was at a loss for words. "I'm sure that your parents would not like to get *another* phone call and . . ."

I groaned. Another phone call would mean I would never get that new bike for Christmas. Another phone call might mean my dad would start looking on the back of matchbook covers for a faraway military school that didn't have vacations.

As Mrs. Pompalini went on and on about being kind to people, I gazed over her left elbow at Mr. Doyle. I guess I would be helping him for another century or two.

"Marsha, we'll talk about this later. You may go line up. . . ." Mrs. Pompalini turned and shook her head at me. "I want you to leave Marsha alone, Roger."

I nodded my head. Yeah, yeah. Go ahead and pin another rap on me. At least I didn't have to go down to the principal's office.

As soon as Mrs. Pompalini left, I went up and tossed my lunch bag in Mr. Doyle's trash can.

"Thanks, Roger." Mr. Doyle was busy picking gum out of the water fountain. He was so serious about his job, as if keeping the school clean was kind of protecting the kids inside.

I was glad no one at school teased him.

Mrs. Pompalini walked up to me. "Roger, it upsets me that you are always getting in trouble. There's nothing wrong with having a sense of humor; you just have to learn when to use it. Practical jokes are not always funny."

"Sorry, Mrs. Pompalini," I said.

Mrs. Pompalini smiled. "And I'm sure you didn't mean to upset Marsha."

I resisted the urge to shout, "But I *love* upsetting Marsha! I try out some of my best routines on that girl."

Patrick hurried over as soon as Mrs. Pompalini left. "Thanks for taking the blame for me, Roger." His ears were bright red.

"No problem, Patrick." I meant it, too. Being yelled at was nothing to me. It might shake up Patrick. "We better leave Marsha alone for a while. If she finds any toads or lizards in her lunch or locker, she might go over the edge." I laughed, picturing Marsha running off into the sunset, pulling her hair out while her eyeballs rolled madly around and around.

"Yeah. We better stay away from her."

"Until January," I said softly.

Patrick grinned. "Until January."

We pulled on our jackets and ran outside. Over by the hedge, the eighth-grade boys were playing basketball. Berry was chomping on a big wad of pink gum and making hoop after hoop. He was the greatest! Why waste any more time thinking about a troublemaker girl like Marsha when you could cheer Berry on?

"Wouldn't it be cool if they asked us to play one day?" asked Patrick.

"It will never happen, Patrick." I had to be honest with him. Only a few seventh-graders were picked to play with the eighth-grade boys.

"Hey, anything can happen, Roger."

"I've had enough happen for one day," I joked. "Besides, until January, when I get my sense of humor out of storage, those eighth-graders won't even know we exist. But, maybe then we can plan some real funny joke on an eighth-grade girl. Maybe a girl that bugs the Berry."

"Yeah!" Patrick gave me a high five. "Plan something great."

"Or, maybe we won't have to wait until January," I said. All of a sudden, I had a great idea. "If we came up with some terrific basketball play, and gave it to Berry, he would have to notice us."

"Yeah," agreed Patrick. "It might help them win the tournament."

"Exactly!" I drew in a deep breath and tried to think. Being funny came easy to me. But maybe thinking up a powerful, foolproof basketball play wouldn't be too hard. Let Sister try to yell at me once I brought Sacred Heart to the basketball finals!

Chapter Six

After recess, while Mrs. Pompalini was writing down our new spelling words, I started scribbling some basketball plays. If I came up with some great ones, Strawberry and his friends might ask me to show them a few moves. Maybe they would ask me to be part of their team for the Best of the Block competition next month.

"Roger?" I looked up. Mrs. Pompalini was pointing her chalk at me. "Have you finished copying your words?"

I looked down at my sheet. It surprised me that I had all the words down.

"Yes," I said.

"Great. Would you go down and get the projector from Mr. Doyle, please?"

Mrs. Pompalini must have picked me to show she still liked me.

Marsha kicked my seat. "Don't get lost, Roger."

I ignored her. I walked down the hall and took the marble stairs two at a time.

"Hey, Roger!" Mr. Doyle always looked so happy to see me. "There's lots of ink marks in the . . . computer room. I hope you get in some more trouble, cause I need some help. You gonna help me, Roger?"

I grinned. "Yeah. I'll see you after school, same as always."

Mr. Doyle leaned over and patted the head of a stuffed squirrel that he had found in the trash can in the Science room. "O-kay. I got me a wit-ness. You're going to help."

Mr. Doyle and I carried the cart and projector upstairs. As we passed the office, I could see our basketball coach talking to Sister Mary Elizabeth.

I slowed down, letting Mr. Doyle push the utility cart down the hall to my classroom. The coach looked upset about something. His face was as red as his hair.

"Look at these: so thin! You can see through them," grumbled Coach Evarts. "The boys are going to be disappointed." He held up a jersey. "I ordered cotton jerseys. These feel like plastic wrap."

Sister nodded. "They aren't very attractive. It's too late to send them back. We're low on funds. I'm sorry, but the P.T.A. spent most of its money on the new printer."

Coach sighed. "Yeah, I guess we're lucky to have these. But after last year's great uniforms, these look second-hand. Too bad we let the kids keep them as a keepsake."

Sister smiled. "Our eighth-graders have talent. We're going to win that competition no matter what they wear."

I wanted to run in and see how bad the jerseys were. Last year, the father of an eighth-grade center had bought jerseys for the whole team, with red warm-up jackets to match.

I hurried to catch up with Mr. Doyle. Luckily we would be watching a film next period. It would give me time to come up with a plan to buy new jerseys for the whole team. I knew how much being on Best of the Block meant to the guys on the team. The older players kept their jerseys straight through high school, especially if their team won that year.

The more I thought about it, the more excited I got. I would get the money, maybe selling some of my mom's cookies door-to-door or washing cars, and then present Strawberry with a check. "Here, Berry. Go pick out something nice. Keep whatever is left over for pizza after the game."

As I raced down the hall I felt goose bumps, picturing the team lifting me to their shoulders and running across the floor, the fans cheering, my parents sitting on freshly scraped bleachers with proud looks on their faces, telling everyone sitting near them, "That's our son!"

All I had to do now was come up with the money.

Chapter Seven

"You're nuts, Roger. There's no way you can come up with that kind of money," Patrick said during lunch the next day.

"Sure I can," I said with a grin. "This is Roger the Dodger you're talking to, Patrick. Getting the team new jerseys is even better than thinking up a basketball play."

"Yeah, well, unless your dad is willing to hand over his Visa card, you'll have to forget this whole idea. It won't work."

Patrick looked so defeated about the whole project, I started to worry myself. "How much do you think new jerseys would cost, Patrick?"

"Well, it would cost about twenty bucks a jersey, times twelve, would be. . . ." Patrick bit into his sandwich and stared up at the ceiling. "Let me see, ten times twelve is one-twenty, so times two would be . . . two hundred and forty dollars." Patrick gulped down his milk, "Plus tax, of course."

My peanut butter sandwich dropped with a dull thwack. "Two hundred and forty dollars!"

"Plus tax."

"I'd have to wash a zillion cars." I pushed my sandwich away and rested my head on the cool table. It smelled like the pine cleaner Mr. Doyle used on the whole school.

"Oh, yippee. Roger's dead!"

I closed my eyes. If I raised my head now I would be too tempted to fling my sandwich at Marsha.

"I guess the rat poison I slipped in his sandwich finally worked," giggled Marsha.

Collette and Marsha started laughing. Marsha was choking on her milk. Even Michael and Freddie were chuckling.

I lifted my head slightly. "Yeah, I noticed some was missing from your cage today, Marsha."

As usual, my rip got the higher rating on the

laugh machine. I sat up, feeling better.

Patrick nudged me with his elbow. "Maybe we could ask for donations. Stand on street corners with tin cans, or send notices home with the kids telling them we need at least a dollar a piece from them."

I thought for a second and then shook my head. "Sister won't let us ask for money unless it's to save a mission or give to Children's Hospital."

Patrick sighed. "So maybe the team can just wear the cheap-looking jerseys."

"I'll think of something," I said. This was Berry's last year at Sacred Heart. He was such a cool guy. I wanted him to have a great jersey to remember us by. He would probably wear it when he appeared on the cover of *Sports Illustrated*. "Yeah, this is my lucky jersey, all right," he would be quoted. "And I have my buddy, Roger Friday, to thank for it."

"What are you smiling about?" Patrick asked.

"Nothing." I got up and gathered my stuff. "Let's figure out how to raise the money."

"It's impossible, Roger. We can't do it."

"Berry and the guys are counting on me, Patrick."

Patrick smiled. "Roger, those guys don't even know who you are."

I was insulted, of course. I reached in my pocket and pulled out my basketball play sheet. "Oh yeah, well, why do I have their secret basketball moves, huh, Mr. Smart Guy?"

Patrick studied the sheet and gave a long, low whistle. "They let you in on their plays?"

Lying to anyone stinks, so I just snatched the sheet back and folded it about thirty times. "I have to show this to the team after school today."

Patrick nodded. "No wonder you want to help the team get new jerseys." He put his hand on my arm. "You're practically their manager."

I tried to look humble.

"Do you think I could help, Roger? I mean, I would be glad to get drinks, or towels, or . . ." Patrick waved his hands in the air. "Maybe keep score. I excel in math. Could you go ask Berry now?"

I glanced over at the eighth-grade table. Berry and his friends were laughing about something. It would be embarrassing if I walked over there and they didn't know who I was. Patrick might be disappointed.

44

"Not now," I said quickly, grabbing my lunch bag. "I'll be seeing them in the gym at three-thirty. I'll talk to Berry in the locker room."

"The locker room," Patrick repeated in awe. "Do you have your own locker, Roger?"

I shook my head.

"Come on," I said. I didn't want to talk anymore about my relationship with the team, especially since I didn't have one.

For the rest of the day I jotted down plans for raising money whenever I finished my work early. By seventh period, I had four wrinkled balls of paper inside my desk and nothing written down in front of me.

"All right, class," said Mrs. Pompalini. "You have thirty minutes to finish your science sheet and put it on my desk."

"Can't we finish it overnight?" asked Patrick.

Lots of kids turned around. Patrick *never* asked for extra time. He was usually the first one finished and already reading a book by the end of class.

"You have thirty minutes, Patrick. That is plenty of time."

"But if we don't finish, will we get a detention or something?"

Mrs. Pompalini laughed. She didn't even answer. I leaned over and poked Patrick with my pencil. He was turning into a real funny man in the making.

A few minutes later, Patrick was rummaging around in his desk. He pulled out a piece of gum, unwrapped it carefully, folded it in half, and slowly stuck it in his mouth.

My mouth fell open. *Nobody* chews gum in Mrs. Pompalini's class. It is one of her pet peeves. And since I had been scraping tons of it myself lately, I was beginning to think it was a pretty smart rule.

Patrick chewed his gum slowly for a while, breaking it in. He rolled his pencil back and forth across his desk, humming a little tune.

"What are you doing?" I hissed.

Patrick looked happy I noticed. He chewed faster.

"Twenty more minutes," called out Mrs. Pompalini.

Patrick put his pencil down. He held up his paper to show me he was only half finished with his science sheet. Even I was on the last question.

Patrick leaned back in his chair and put his hands behind his head like he was sitting on the beach. He chomped down hard on his gum.

I dropped my own pencil on the floor and when I bent down to pick it up, I tugged on Patrick's leg. "What do you think you're doing, Patrick?"

Patrick smiled and tried to wink. Either that or some gum had sprayed up in his eye. At the rate he was chomping, he was liable to snap off his tongue.

A few kids turned around and stared at Patrick. You could see how shocked they were right away. Chomping gum and acting like a smart aleck just wasn't like Patrick. It was not a natural state of affairs. It was like seeing Sister Mary Elizabeth stealing from the poor box.

Mrs. Pompalini was busy at the blackboard listing the English homework. As soon as she turned around she would notice Patrick. Patrick was acting like he wanted to get caught. He certainly wasn't chewing it in a sly, let-me-see-if-I-can-get-away-with-it kind of way. Patrick was chomping, smacking, and cracking it. He might as well have worn a look-at-me-I'm-chewing-gum sign.

Mrs. Pompalini set down her chalk and dusted off her fingertips. She brushed back her hair and sat down. It wasn't until Patrick blew a bubble the size of a grapefruit that Mrs. Pompalini looked up.

"Patrick, my goodness," she said. "Please put that gum in the trash can this minute."

Patrick looked over at me and grinned. I wanted to rush over and put my hand on his forehead to see if he was burning up with some mysterious fever. Maybe his brain was on fire.

When Mrs. Pompalini looked back down at her desk, Patrick looked so disappointed, I thought he was going to cry. I was shocked when he leaned forward and blew two quick bubbles in a row, ending each with a crisp crack.

When Mrs. Pompalini looked up, Patrick pulled the end of the gum out of his mouth and stretched it out a good foot.

"Patrick Frank!" Mrs. Pompalini's neck flushed red. "I told you to throw away your gum, young man."

After a few more ear-shattering smacks, Patrick leaned forward. "I don't want to throw my gum away, Mrs. Pompalini. It makes me happy."

I groaned. Mrs. Pompalini stood up, her cheeks spotty red. The whole class was staring at Patrick. Even I leaned closer. Talk about guts!

Mrs. Pompalini looked worried now. "Are you all right, Patrick?"

"Fine, thanks," replied Patrick. "And you?"

A few kids giggled.

"I am getting angry, Patrick. Now put the gum in the trash *this minute*."

Patrick leaned back in his seat and blew a bubble. I covered my eyes. This was getting too rich for my blood.

When I looked up, Patrick's name was on the board under detention, right below mine. He was standing by the trash can, rolling his pink wad of gum into a scrap of paper.

"Sorry, Mrs. Pompalini," said Patrick sincerely. "I don't know what came over me."

Mrs. Pompalini looked relieved.

"Go down to the office and ask your mother to pick you up at five, Patrick," said Mrs. Pompalini. "Rules are rules."

On the way back to his desk, Patrick passed mine. As he walked by, he tossed a small white square of paper on my desk. My hand slammed down on it fast. I didn't know if Patrick was trying for a double detention or what, but I knew how Mrs. Pompalini felt about note writing in her class.

It wasn't until the bell rang that I slid the note into my lap and unfolded it.

ROGER,
I'VE GOT A PLAN.
PATRICK

Chapter Eight

Mr. Doyle was so happy to have Patrick helping, he gave him his best putty knife. Patrick was pretty happy himself. He hadn't stopped grinning since the buses left.

"I wanted to meet the team, Roger," Patrick had explained on the way down to Mr. Doyle's office. "I think I have a plan for raising money for the new jerseys."

"What?" My heart was beating faster. If Patrick raised the money, then Berry and the guys on the team would be carrying *him* around on their shoulders instead of me.

"Simple," Patrick laughed. "We sell programs. In advance."

The idea sounded good, but no one would pay more than a nickel for the ditto sheets that Coach Evarts usually passed out. At a nickel a program we would have to sell fifty or sixty thousand. Since I wasn't as accurate in math as Patrick, I kept my rough estimate to myself.

"The programs aren't that hot, Patrick. Will we sell enough?"

"Not the old ones," admitted Patrick. "But the new ones I'll set up on my computer will be great. Then we can go around and ask for advertisers like they do on the back of the church bulletin. They'll pay us twenty bucks to have their name on the back of the Best of the Block."

"Cool." The idea made a lot of sense. "We could call our advertisers the Best Businesses on the Block."

"Yeah, that's a great idea, Roger. We would only have to get twelve stores."

"Or maybe thirteen." Maybe I could get myself a jersey.

Patrick yanked open the gym door and marched inside. We both stopped and watched the basketball team going through its drill. All twelve players were working on their shooting.

"Do you want to tell them, or should I?" asked Patrick.

"It was your idea," I said fairly. "Go ahead."

Patrick nodded, tapping the putty knife against his hand. "But *you* are their best friend."

I nodded, wondering if maybe we should just write the team a letter. I could tape my school picture to the bottom so they would know which kid to pick up and put on their shoulders when they won the game.

A loud whistle stopped the drills and made Patrick drop his putty knife. Coach Evarts blasted it again and walked into the middle of the gym. He let the big cardboard box he was carrying drop to the floor.

"Okay guys, listen up." He bent down and grabbed a jersey from the box. "The jerseys for the Best of the Block came in this morning."

Berry and Eddie Jamison slapped each other a high-five.

"Let's see," said a lot of the kids. Even Gym Rat left his wall position and walked over slowly to take a look.

"We are going to look so fine!" said a kid named Rick. "Let me see those jerseys."

"Do we get to keep them?" asked another kid.

"Sure, my brother got to keep his!" laughed Eddie. "Do we have our names on the front or back, Coach?"

Coach Evarts held up the jersey. All of the laughing and whistling stopped. The jersey hung limply in his hands. It was so thin I could see the disappointed face of Berry-the-Strawberry right through the pale mesh.

"I thought the jerseys would be a little thicker," Coach explained. "But at least we have something. These will be okay."

Eddie scratched his head. "Last year the jerseys were so cool."

"No offense, Coach," said a stocky kid with curly hair. "But our gym shirts are better than these."

Coach Evarts dropped the jersey back in the box. "But four of you go to Central, six go to Sacred Heart, and there are two more from Peabody. Come on, guys, help me out here. We have to dress the same."

Patrick nudged me. "Tell them your plan."

"It's *your* plan," I whispered back. "You tell them."

"They know you," Patrick shot back.

"Yo, coach." It was Gym Rat. He picked up a jersey and shook his head. "I can get you a deal on some jerseys."

Berry shot a basketball toward Gym Rat. Rat was startled at first, but he caught the ball easily.

"What kind of deal?"

Gym Rat shrugged. "You come up with some coin and I'll make sure you guys look good," He gave a short laugh. "Might take the fans longer to realize you can't play as well as you think."

Eddie reached out and gave him a little shove. "Hey, I don't see you on this team, Rattner."

"I didn't want to play with kids," Gym Rat said. "I've got better things to do."

Coach held up his hands. "Guys, grow up, okay." He gave the cardboard box a little nudge with his shoe. "Grab a jersey, keep track of it, and just be glad you have something, okay?"

Strawberry was the first to bend down and pick one up. "Thanks, Coach." He pulled it on over his T-shirt. It was a little tight across his chest. "This will be fine."

Another kid picked one up. "Yeah, it's cool."

Strawberry bent down and started tossing the

shirts to other kids on the team. "It's the man in the shirt, bud, not the shirt on the man."

Patrick and I both nodded.

Eddie and his friend, Bob, caught their jerseys in midair, but didn't put them on. Eddie just looked down at his and shook his head.

Mr. Doyle came in then, pushing his cart. "It's time, boys."

Patrick followed Mr. Doyle to the left side of the gym. I watched as Coach Evarts picked up the empty box and started to walk off the court.

"Hey, Coach!" I was halfway across the court before I realized I didn't know what I was going to say. After watching Strawberry being so great about everything, I knew I wanted to do something.

Coach stopped.

"I think I might have a plan to get some new jerseys." My voice seemed to echo in the big gym.

"Yeah, you and who else?" said Gym Rat with a smirk.

"Me!" said Patrick from across the gym. He gave a little wave to the team. "I helped formulate the original plan."

"Who sent for the Boy Scouts of America?" laughed Eddie.

"You kids planning on cracking open your piggy banks?" laughed Bob.

Coach blasted his whistle. "Give it a rest." He turned and smiled at me. "What's your name, kid?"

Even from across the room, I could see the surprise on Patrick's face.

"It's me, Roger, Rog . . ." I shrugged. "You know, Roger-the-Dodger?"

"Roger-the-WHAT?" laughed Eddie. "Did you fall out of some Hardy Boy novel, kid?"

Strawberry bounced the basketball to me. "Hey, ignore them, Richie. Tell us your plan."

"Roger . . . it's Roger." I turned my back a little, not wanting to see Patrick's face.

Strawberry smiled and nodded. "Yeah, Roger-the-Dodger. That's cool."

Coach Evarts glanced up at the clock. "We better hustle." He pointed his whistle at me. "You wanted to say something, kid?"

"Yeah. My friend Patrick and I thought if we sold advertising space on the back of the program for the Best of the Block, and then charged a dollar a program, it would raise some money and you guys could get nicer jerseys."

Patrick was by my side in a second. "I mean, these jerseys are okay, but if we had the money anyway . . ."

"We could ask twenty dollars for a half page ad," I suggested.

"Or ten dollars and we could ask twenty-four stores to chip in," added Patrick. "Or maybe sell quarter-page ads for five dollars to forty-eight stores."

Gym Rat jerked his thumb toward us. "Who are these kids, anyway? I feel like I'm stuck in the middle of a *Brady Bunch* rerun."

Strawberry took a step closer to us. "Hey, clam up, okay? Let's hear what they want to say."

Gym Rat's face looked hurt before it changed to anger. "I already offered to help. My uncle happens to own a sports shop, and . . ."

"Save it, Rattner," said another kid. "You just want to drum up some business for your uncle."

"Quiet!" Coach Evarts grabbed the ball basket and started tossing the balls out to the players. "I really don't care what you guys wear for the game. You're acting like a bunch of crybabies right now and if I have to listen to any more of this garbage, I'm walking and you won't be playing for anyone, wearing anything at all."

The gym was absolutely still. Finally Strawberry started dribbling the basketball. "Sorry, Coach. Come on, guys, let's get back to work."

Patrick and I started off the court. Rattner followed us.

"Guess your big hero routine didn't pan out so well, did it, kids?" he snickered.

"So what?" said Patrick. But his ears were bright red.

I turned around to say something to Rattner, but he was already leaning against the wall. He didn't look mean then. He had the same look on his face a kid wears when he's the very last person picked during gym class.

"So," I said, walking over to the bleachers and jabbing at a large purple lump. "I guess I exaggerated a little. The team and I aren't so close."

Patrick jabbed at a pink wad and shrugged. Then he looked up and smiled. "What's that, Richie?"

We both laughed.

I was sailing a huge lump of gum toward Mr.

Doyle's can when a kid in a high school jacket walked in and leaned against the wall next to Rattner. I was glad he had some friends. They both left the gym.

"You workers need a soda break?" asked Mr. Doyle. He reached in his pocket and pulled out some quarters. "Let me unlock the teachers' room." He unclipped the huge key ring from his belt. "The key with the T taped to it is the one. See boys? All my keys have a tag."

"You're real organized," I said.

"That's me, all right," agreed Mr. Doyle.

"Boy, detention is great," whispered Patrick. "Mr. Doyle is so nice to us."

"Yeah," I whispered back. "Free sodas and the best seat in the house to watch the basketball team practice."

We were halfway out the door when the Best of the Block started acting their worst.

Chapter Nine

The three of us spun around as one. Noise, whistles, and shouting filled the gym. I couldn't believe it when Strawberry took one of the water bottles and squirted Eddie right in the face.

"You need to cool down, Maitland," laughed Strawberry.

"You idiot!" shouted Eddie. "You need to know when to quit, man." His fist sailed toward Strawberry.

Strawberry tried to duck, but Eddie's knuckles grazed his right cheek.

"Hey, what's wrong with you?" cried Strawberry. He touched his face gingerly, then stared down at the blood on his hand.

"You watch what you're saying about my brother. You hear me?"

"He didn't say beans about your brother," shouted Bob. "Berry just said we were going to make last year's team look weak."

Eddie's face flushed red. "Yeah, well my brother was *on* that team. Nobody plays better than Jake. He dunked five baskets during that game. You guys couldn't dunk if they lowered the basket three feet."

Coach Evarts ran over. "What is going on here? Seems I can't look away for a second."

Strawberry held up both hands. "I have no idea what set this guy off, Coach."

"I just told you!" shouted Eddie. "You think you're such a jock and — "

Coach blasted his whistle. "It's over. Now if there is one more outburst like this, you two are out of the Best of the Block. You hear me? The whole idea of the contest is to get players from other schools to play as one team." Coach glanced at Eddie and Strawberry and shook his head. "And you two seem to get in a fight every day about something."

"Eddie has a short fuse, Coach," said Bob.

"Shut up, Patterson," cried Eddie.

"Everyone shut up," ordered Coach Evarts. "Look at this floor. Someone is going to slip and break an ankle."

"Eddie's *neck* if we're lucky," snickered Bob.

Coach shot Bob a withering glance.

"Sorry," said Bob, ducking his head.

Coach took a step closer and examined Strawberry's cheek. "Better put some ice on that."

"He started it," said Eddie.

Mr. Doyle took Patrick's and my arm and led us over to the group. "No, Eddie. You was the one."

Eddie scowled. "Who asked you?"

My heart stopped for a second. If Eddie dared to insult Mr. Doyle, I'd be tempted to hit him myself.

"We saw the whole thing, right, boys?" said Mr. Doyle. He held up his keys. "I'll unlock the nurse's office, Berry."

"And get a mop for this floor, Mr. Doyle," Coach said. "We're going to end up with a team full of injuries."

"Okay, okay," said Mr. Doyle. He glanced at Strawberry and then at the floor. "Maybe I better clean up the floor."

I put my hand on the keys. "I'll unlock the door to the nurse's office, Mr. Doyle. I know where the ice packs are and everything."

Mr. Doyle kept a firm grip on the keys. He frowned and shook his head. "Maybe you can get the mop, boys. I'm in charge of the keys."

Berry used the bottom of his shirt to wipe his cheek. It was really bleeding bad now.

"I don't know where the mops are," I said quickly. Berry was already starting to walk away. Patrick was following him, motioning for me to hurry up. "It's okay, Mr. Doyle. I'm practically your assistant. You can trust me."

Mr. Doyle looked over at Coach Evarts. Coach kept tapping his fingers on his clipboard. "Somebody, please get a mop."

"Okay," Mr. Doyle said slowly. "You unlock it with the key with an N, Roger. Then you lock up and bring me back my keys, okay?"

"Sure," I said, snatching the keys and racing across the gym floor. "Be right back, Mr. Doyle."

I caught up with Patrick and Berry by the office.

I let Patrick unlock the nurse's door, but I was the one who filled up the ice pack and handed it to Berry. Berry even listened to me when I told him to lie down on the green couch until the bleeding stopped. After a few minutes, I was able to stick a huge square bandage on it. Luckily I was able to find one that didn't have little rabbits on it.

"Feels a lot better," Berry said. "Eddie must have clipped me with his ring."

With just the three of us in the nurse's office, it felt as though Patrick and I were Berry's private trainers.

"Better get back to practice." He flicked off the lights and we all walked out the door. "Thanks for the help, guys."

"Anytime," Patrick offered. "I mean, I hope you don't get socked every day, but if you do, you can count on us."

"Great." Berry grinned at us. "I'll remember that."

Halfway down the hall, Berry stopped. "Hey, you know what? Maybe you guys can help us the day of the tournament. I'll double check with the coach, but I'm sure it will be okay. Yesterday he asked if anyone knew someone who might want to help fill up water bottles, run for towels, be in charge of the basketballs."

"Cool!" Patrick and I said together.

"Can we sit on the bench with the team?" I asked.

Berry nodded and started laughing. "Sure! As long as it's not on my lap."

"Wow!" mumbled Patrick. "Wait till the kids hear about this."

Berry hurried on ahead, turning at the door to give us one final wave.

"We're lucky, Patrick." I dribbled an imaginary basketball and arced it over the water fountain. "Three points."

I tossed the ball to Patrick, who dribbled it twice, then hooped it near the wall clock.

"We'll be sitting on the bench with them," said Patrick. "They'll all know our names by the end of the game."

"We better wear name tags, just in case. Otherwise they'll call me Richie," I suggested.

An alarm went off in my head when I heard the word tag! Mr. Doyle tagged all of his keys! I stuck my hands in my pockets. "Hey, Patrick, do you have the keys?"

Patrick spun around, already heading down the hall. "I left them in the door. I'll be right back."

Waiting for Patrick to run back up the hall, jingling the keys, was the longest three minutes of my life. Patrick returned with the keys in a minute. But even then it wasn't soon enough.

Chapter Ten

The next morning I woke up in a terrific mood. I could hardly wait to get to school to tell the whole fifth grade Patrick and I were the new managers of the Best of the Block. My imagination was running wild. Mental pictures flashed through my mind: Berry insisting Patrick and I eat lunch with him, Coach Evarts presenting us with silver whistles, or Eddie and Bob insisting Patrick and I shoot some hoops during recess.

I had good news for Coach Evarts, too. My dad liked the idea of selling ads for the program so much, he was willing to help collect the ads. My hand closed around the check for ten dollars in my pocket. Our first ad was from my dad. THANK

GOODNESS THERE'S FRIDAY WHEN YOUR PIPES FREEZE ON THURSDAY! FRIDAY PLUMBING 555-3150.

But before I had time to share any of my good news, I heard about the *bad* news. The night before, someone had broken into the school's computer room and stolen the new laser printer.

I hurried up the front steps of Sacred Heart. When had the thief struck? Patrick and I had stayed until five. Mr. Doyle said he was going to stay another hour or two.

As soon as I walked into the school, I saw a policeman in the office, talking to Sister Mary Elizabeth. Miss Merkle was talking on the phone and Mr. Doyle was slumped in a chair, his hands clenched together on his lap.

I reached behind me and pulled Patrick up the last step. "Look. Mr. Doyle is in the office. Do you think the thief tried to rob him, too?"

"Mr. Doyle might *be* the robber," said a big kid beside me. He shoved his glasses up a notch and jerked his thumb toward the office. "Sister called my mom this morning to let her know what happened since my mom is the president of the P.T.A. Mr. Doyle was the only one who had a key to the computer room. And Mr. Doyle keeps saying that he didn't lose his key ring, but *someone* had the key to the computer room. Sounds kind of fishy to me."

I elbowed the big kid in the leg and frowned. "Yeah, well you *smell* kind of fishy to me. Everyone knows Mr. Doyle would never steal."

The kid shrugged. "Hey, all I know is what my mom told my dad at breakfast this morning."

Patrick crossed his arms. "Gossip can't be used in a court of law. Is your mom a cop or something?"

"I told you she's president of the P.T.A., which is even more important than being a cop. She organized the book sale and the spaghetti dinner that raised the thousand bucks to buy the laser printer. So, my mom knows more than you do."

The back of my neck was getting hot. "Yeah, well my dog knows more than you. So what?"

"So, if Mr. Doyle and Sister are the only two who have a set of keys to the computer room, *one* of them messed up. Because the thief didn't have to break in."

"Mr. Doyle always keeps his keys with him," I insisted.

70

Patrick grabbed my arm. "The nurse's office!"

The keys! Patrick and I stared at each other.

He and I knocked against each other as we tried to push through the office door. Patrick slumped into a chair by the door, but I hurried closer and stood by the water cooler. Since I was in the office so much, no one even noticed.

"My keys were upstairs in the convent, officer," explained Sister. "Are you sure the thief had a key?"

The policeman nodded. "There was no forcible entry. Now maybe the door was left unlocked."

Mr. Doyle looked up. "No, sir. That door was locked. I cleaned the computer room real good and then I locked the door."

"Are you *absolutely* sure you had the keys with you when you left the building, Mr. Doyle?" asked Sister Mary Elizabeth.

I cringed, embarrassed for Mr. Doyle. I could tell by the tone of Sister's voice that she had already asked him the same question a hundred times.

Mr. Doyle nodded. "Yes, Sister. I had my keys. I locked the front door of the school, and then I took the bus home. Same as always."

Sister sat on the edge of her desk and sighed. "Well, I can't understand how the thief got in."

Mr. Doyle patted his keys. "Here are my keys. My keys always stay with me. Right on my belt."

I stared at the keys, fear starting to swirl in my stomach. Had Mr. Doyle forgotten that he let me have the keys to unlock the nurse's office yesterday? When I glanced over at Patrick he was looking as sick as I felt. Did Mr. Doyle mention giving us the keys, or was he trying to keep us out of trouble?

I leaned my head against the water cooler, wondering if I should just offer the information myself. Or would that get Mr. Doyle in more trouble?

"Roger!" Sister hopped off her desk and pulled me out from behind the cooler. "Roger, you are just the person I wanted to talk to."

"Me?" I squeaked.

Sister put her arm around my shoulder and led me to the policeman. Another two steps and she would toss me to the officer, crying, "Lock him up at once. He has had more detention than any fifth-grader in America. He stole the laser printer, too."

"Roger's the boy I have been telling you about, officer," explained Sister.

My hands started to sweat. I could see Patrick sinking lower and lower in his chair. Any second now and his body would disappear from view. It was going to be me alone in the county jail!

"There has been a theft in the computer room, Roger," said Sister. "You were with Mr. Doyle until five last night. Do you remember Mr. Doyle setting the keys down?"

Sister was talking in a real slow, loud voice, as if Mr. Doyle and I were zombie twins. I hate it when people do that to Mr. Doyle. He can't talk fast, and he doesn't sit around his office reading *The Wall Street Journal,* but he is smart in lots of important ways, like being nice to everyone he talks to.

The policeman flipped his notebook page over and licked the tip of his pencil. "Mr. Doyle, did you ever leave the keys in your office for even a few minutes? Maybe when you were washing up to leave for the day?"

"Morning, everyone!" Strawberry knocked twice on the office door as he walked by. Sister smiled briefly and nodded at Strawberry, then looked back at Mr. Doyle.

"Hi, Berry," called out Mr. Doyle. He touched his cheek. "Hey, Roger. How's Berry's cheek?"

Before I could even say a word, Mr. Doyle stood straight up, his eyes opened wide. "Oh, my."

"Mr. Doyle," I cried. "It's my fault, not yours."

Sister and the policeman stared at each other and then me. Patrick groaned from his chair and covered his eyes.

"No, no, Roger," said Mr. Doyle. He fumbled with his key ring, taking it off his belt and fumbling with key after key. "Sister, I think I know what happened."

"What?" Sister asked.

"Here's the office key, the art room key, the gym key . . ." Mr. Doyle kept licking his lips and flipping through his key ring. "Oh, my. I can't find it. It's not here on my ring. It should be here."

The policeman took the ring from Mr. Doyle and flipped through the keys. "What's wrong?"

"The computer key must be missing," said Sister, taking the keys from the policeman. "Mr. Doyle has it tagged with a C."

"It's all my fault," I cried. "Berry got hurt and

74

I had to unlock the nurse's room. I forgot to take the keys out of the door. As soon as we got to the gym, we remembered and raced back. The keys were still in the door so we thought no big deal, but I guess, if the computer key is missing . . ." I stopped to swallow. "I guess maybe the thief stole the computer key off the ring and left the others so no one would get suspicious, and . . ."

"Stop!" ordered Sister. "Slow down, Roger. Who is this *we* you keep talking about? You and Mr. Doyle?"

I drew in a deep breath and shook my head. I kept my head down, unable to meet Mr. Doyle's confused face or the terror in the eyes of Patrick.

"Then who?" asked Sister quietly. "Tell me who was with you when you left the keys in the door."

I sighed, wishing I had never, ever brought that dead snake to school, wishing Marsha had never screamed her head off, wishing I had never ended up getting detention, and most of all wishing I had remembered to take the keys out of the nurse's door so Mr. Doyle wouldn't be in so much trouble. But, it was too late for wishes. It was too late for anything but the truth.

75

Chapter Eleven

The policeman took a step closer to me. "All right now, Roger, who was with you? No lies now."

"Roger doesn't lie," Sister said quietly. "Tell the policeman what you know. Who was with you, Roger?"

I closed my eyes, wishing I could lie. I wanted to take the blame. I certainly deserved it.

But they wanted the truth.

"Patrick," I said.

"Patrick Frank?" From the surprised look on Sister's face, you would have thought I had said the Pope.

Patrick scrambled to his feet, tightening the

knot of his plaid tie. "It can be explained very quickly, Sister." Patrick smiled at the policeman. "You see, there was a fight in the gym and Berry got punched."

"What?" Sister sat back down on her desk. "Where was Coach Evarts?"

"He was there, and he did a good job yelling at everyone," I added. "Then he asked Mr. Doyle to hurry up and get a mop to clean up the water . . ."

"And Berry was bleeding, so Roger and I offered to run down to the nurse's office and get some ice," continued Patrick. "So, we did, and then we forgot that the keys were still in the door. So I ran back down the hall and took them out and gave them to Mr. Doyle."

Sister frowned. "Mr. Doyle should have never given you boys the keys in the first place."

Mr. Doyle nodded. "I should have told Roger where I kept my mops. But, the mops had just been washed. Then I hung them on high hooks in the furnace room. Roger is too short."

I tried to shrink myself even more, to let Sister know that I never could have reached those mops.

The policeman started writing in his notebook. "Okay, well at least this is starting to make sense.

How long were the keys left in the door?"

"Two minutes," I said.

Patrick shook his head. "Well, not really. We left them in the door and then took care of Berry. I'd say more like ten minutes."

"Ten minutes?" cried Sister. "That's long enough for anyone in the building to come and take them off the ring."

"I didn't hear anyone," I said quickly.

Sister frowned. "Thieves don't wear bells, Roger."

"I'll need a list of everyone who was in the building during those ten minutes," said the policeman. "The coach, his players, anyone else serving detention."

"I'll have that for you within the hour, Officer Jones," promised Sister.

"Okay." The policeman closed his notebook and slipped it into his back pocket. "I'll wait for the list. While I'm here, I'll go talk to the coach. In the meantime, keep track of your own computer room key."

Sister glanced at her desk. "I will keep the computer room key with me."

Mr. Doyle nodded. "Maybe I can make a copy,

78

Sister. So I can have one on my key ring. Same as always."

Sister flushed red, but she shook her head. "Let's just wait until we get this cleared up, Mr. Doyle."

I felt like crying. Keys meant a lot to Mr. Doyle. They let him know he was important to Sacred Heart.

"Should we contact an attorney?" Patrick asked.

The officer grinned. "Nah. We'll work this out. I have the feeling someone here at the school took the printer. Maybe we'll get lucky and find out who."

"It wasn't Mr. Doyle," I cried.

Mr. Doyle jerked his head up, shocked. "They know that, Roger."

I hoped they did. Because if anyone tried to arrest Mr. Doyle, they would have to take me, too.

Chapter Twelve

By afternoon, the entire school knew the laser printer had been stolen. Some kids were even saying that Miss Merkle's typewriter had been taken, too. A first-grader announced to the whole cafeteria that the robber stole the whole church.

Sister Mary Elizabeth asked Patrick and me not to mention anything that had been said in her office, especially about the keys being left in the door of the nurse's office. But, the story leaked out somehow. Maybe somebody saw Patrick and me in the office, because kids I barely knew kept coming up to us at lunch, asking all sorts of questions.

Usually, I like attention. But not this kind. It didn't make me feel a bit famous. Now I knew how embarrassed the people feel who end up on the covers of those papers my mom won't let me read at the supermarket.

Like when a sixth-grader came over and asked me if I had sold the computer room key to the thief.

"Yes, Mr. Detective. I sold the key for a million dollars, which is why my whole lunch bag is stuffed with one dollar bills."

Most of the kids at my table just laughed.

"So why were you in the principal's office so long then?" continued Mr. Detective. "Explain that!"

I shrugged. "I was trying to sell Sister an advertisement for the basketball program."

"Oh, yeah," said the detective. "Sure!"

"She loved my ideas," I said. "BECOME A NUN; IT'S FUN!"

Patrick choked on his milk. He hadn't touched a bite of his sandwich. A life of crime was really upsetting his system. He wiped his chin and tried to smile. It wasn't any use. Maybe I wasn't even that funny anymore.

Why had I been so stupid about leaving the keys in the door? What if Mr. Doyle got fired because of my mistake? If the president of the P.T.A. got mad enough, she could cause a lot of trouble for Mr. Doyle.

When the sixth-grade detective got bored trying to scare us, Patrick leaned over and elbowed me.

"So, Roger," he whispered. "What are we going to do to help Mr. Doyle?"

"We have to do something," I agreed. "Did you notice he didn't even get mad at us? He told Sister that we were the best two helpers he's ever had."

"We might be the *last* two helpers he ever had," pointed out Patrick.

I didn't even want to think of Mr. Doyle leaving Sacred Heart. "I guess there's only one thing to do, Patrick."

"What?"

I crumpled up my lunch bag and smiled. "Catch the real thief."

Patrick did not return my smile. "Are you crazy?"

I stood up and made a small bow. "Just about."

Patrick stood up, too, grabbing my arm and pushing me up the aisle toward the trash cans. "Listen, Roger, let me remind you of a few important facts. Number one: we are only ten years old. Fifth-graders cannot crack police cases that stump forty-year-old cops. Number two: If we try to catch the thief, we will only end up in more trouble. And once my mom finds out I'm partly responsible for the stolen laser printer, she will send me to military school so I won't ruin my whole life. And number three: Once — "

I groaned. "I've heard enough, Patrick. I don't want you throwing away your career of being President of the United States, just to clear Mr. Doyle's name."

"It isn't that," insisted Patrick. "I want to clear Mr. Doyle's name just as much as you do. The point is, we won't be able to catch the thief."

"I disagree."

"Me, too."

I jumped a foot. I knew that voice. Usually it was shrieking, higher pitched, and filled with rage, but I recognized it right away.

"Marsha!" I said, trying to appear relaxed. This was hard to do since Marsha normally ties my nervous system into a frazzled knot. "How long have you been listening to this private, personal, and none-of-your-business conversation?"

Marsha tossed back her hair. "It *is* my business,

Roger. You're not the only one who likes Mr. Doyle. I want to help."

"What are you talking about? Patrick and I were just talking about his political career. And frankly, Marsha, voting for him in another ten or twenty years is all the help we need from you."

Marsha gave me a dirty look and took a step closer to Patrick. "Patrick, let me help you find the thief. I don't want Mr. Doyle to get in trouble. Lots of kids are saying that Mr. Doyle lost his keys and by the time he found them, the thief had already stolen the printer."

"Not exactly," I blurted out. "Your facts, like your head, are full of holes."

"Be quiet, Roger. Mr. Doyle is innocent," Marsha continued. "He's so honest and nice. When I lost my First Holy Communion pin at the church, my very own mother gave up looking for it after an hour. But Mr. Doyle kept looking and looking and he called us *three* hours later to tell us he found it." Marsha's eyes got all shiny. "And he wouldn't even take the twenty-dollar reward that my dad tried to give him."

Even though Marsha drives me bonkers, I almost liked her then.

84

"Don't worry, Marsha. Mrs. Pompalini thinks they will catch the real thief," said Patrick.

"That will take too long," said Marsha.

"I agree," I said.

"I have a plan," Marsha whispered. "Don't tell anyone because it will only work if it's kept a secret."

Patrick and I nodded.

Marsha raised her left arm and pushed back her sleeve. A thin gold bracelet with two rows of tiny diamonds sparkled under the bright cafeteria lights.

"Whoa, who won the lottery?" I grabbed Marsha's arm and took a closer look. "Are you going to sell this and use the money for a good attorney for Mr. Doyle?"

Marsha snatched back her arm. "No, dummy. When the thief sees my expensive, but fake, diamond bracelet he'll try to steal it. He won't be able to resist it."

Patrick grinned. "Yeah, and then we'll nab him."

Marsha beamed. "That's right. We'll be heroes."

"Yeah," I growled. "Unless the thief decides to

shoot us all in our pointed heads. Then we'll be dead."

Marsha frowned. "You're just jealous because I thought up the plan. Besides, Roger, a bullet would just bounce off your hard head."

"Better a *hard* head than an *empty* one like yours," I snapped back.

"Be quiet, you two," ordered Patrick. "Fighting is wasting time."

Marsha and I both stared at Patrick. The kid never lost his temper. Especially at me, his best friend.

"I think Marsha's plan is good," Patrick said. "But we have to be careful. We have to set the trap in a safe place, like here at school."

"School is a dangerous place for me," I reminded Patrick. "I never know when Sister is going to pounce on me and slap on another detention. If I get in any more trouble my parents are going to send me to live with Gramma Olenski for the next twenty years."

Patrick grinned. "Gramma Olenski?"

"Yeah, Gramma Olenski. You met her last summer at our Fourth of July party, Patrick. Gramma's idea of raising children is that they are never seen, heard, or fed."

Patrick and I laughed. Gramma made Sister seem like a stand-up comic.

"There isn't time for jokes," reminded Marsha. She put her hands on her hips and tapped her foot. The lady was all business. "Here's my plan. After school, I'll walk into the gym and pretend I'm asking you two a question about homework. Then I'll push up my sleeves and let everyone see my bracelet. Patrick, you say something like, 'Hey, Marsha, you better be *real careful* about wearing that diamond bracelet.' "

Patrick reached into his pocket and pulled out a scrap of paper. He pulled a pen from his shirt pocket and started scribbling his lines. "Okay, maybe I can even say, 'Marsha, why don't you put the bracelet someplace safe?' "

Marsha smiled. "Great."

"What's *great* about it?" I wanted to know. "The basketball team is going to wonder why you don't just go home and put it in your jewelry box."

Marsha snapped her fingers. "You're right."

Too bad I didn't have a tape recorder. I knew

it would be the only time in my life Marsha Cessano would admit I was right about something.

"I'll pretend I'm staying after to help correct papers," said Marsha. "No, wait. I need a dirtier job."

"Try looking at yourself in the mirror," I suggested with a small smile.

Patrick and Marsha ignored me.

"Marsha, announce that you're helping Sister clean the old copy machine in the office," said Patrick. "It's always a mess."

"Perfect!" Marsha beamed at Patrick. "No wonder you get A's all the time. You are *so* smart."

Patrick blushed. I gagged. Patrick was treating Marsha like she was actually human.

"Then," continued Marsha. "I'll say I am going to put the bracelet in a safe place. Once I leave, you two follow and we'll all hide until the thief sneaks in to steal it." Marsha patted Patrick on the shoulder. "We'll have three witnesses. That should be enough for Sister and the police."

"Wait a second, troops," I interrupted. "Exactly *where* are the three witnesses going to be hiding?"

Marsha shrugged. "In the girl's locker room, of

course. The shower room is huge."

I groaned. Great! If I got caught hiding in the girl's shower, I would bypass Gramma Olenski and automatically go to jail.

"I don't know," Patrick began nervously. "Can't we hide the bracelet in the *boy's* locker room, Marsha?"

"What would I be doing in the boy's locker room?" snapped Marsha.

"Erasing your name?" I suggested.

Marsha socked me hard on the arm. Her fake diamond bracelet twinkled as she delivered the punch.

"So what's your plan, Roger?" asked Marsha.

"Announce that you are going to put the bracelet in your locker," I suggested.

"Yeah. Locker G 108!"

"And we can all hide in the supply closet and watch," said Patrick.

"Okay. It's worth a try," I admitted. "Will your mom let you stay after school today, Marsha?"

Marsha smiled. "My mom loves it when I offer to help Sister in the office. I'll help Sister for ten minutes and then come down to the gym."

"It's a date," Patrick said cheerfully.

"No, it isn't," I grumbled. The thought of my best friend and my worst enemy hitting it off so nicely was giving me a headache the size of a basketball.

Basketball!

All of a sudden, I started to get worried. The only people scheduled to be in the gym besides Coach Evarts was the Best of the Block team.

What if the thief turned out to be one of the players?

Chapter Thirteen

Marsha insisted on walking around the playground with Patrick and me so we could discuss possible suspects. This idea was not appealing. The whole school was already talking about us. If they saw me strolling along with Marsha, who knew what headlines were possible?

ROGER FRIDAY AND MARSHA CESSANO SEEN WALKING ARM AND ARM AFTER LUNCH. SPRING WEDDING PLANNED.

I turned up the collar on my jacket and avoided the basketball area where Berry and his friends hung out.

"First of all," said Marsha. "Let's think of all the guys who were in the gym right before you two left with the keys. Tell me the names of all the troublemaking kids on the team."

I bit my lip. I didn't want to get innocent kids in trouble. There was a difference between a smart mouth and a mean kid. I should know.

"I can't believe we left the keys in the door," mumbled Patrick.

I glared at Patrick. He had told Marsha every measly detail of the case. He even told her Berry had asked us both to be team managers. If I had a cork, I would have popped it in his mouth before he leaked out a few more secrets.

I glanced over at the eight-grade section of the playground. Berry trusted me, and here I was trying to set a trap for someone on the team. It was hard to think of Berry having anything to do with stealing the printer.

Turning in a player would be hard. Maybe impossible. But Mr. Doyle's name had to be cleared.

Marsha tugged on my arm. "You aren't listening to me, Roger. I asked you who else was in the gym yesterday."

"What's that kid's last name?" asked Patrick. "The one who was giving the team a hard time?"

"Jimmy Rattner," I said. "Only he left the gym

with some other kid before Mr. Doyle gave us the keys."

"Ha!" hooted Marsha. "Maybe they didn't leave the building. Did anything else happen?"

"There was the fight between Eddie and Berry," said Patrick. "That's why we had to unlock the nurse's office."

Marsha smiled. "Maybe Eddie stole the printer. If he's mean enough to hit Berry, he must be horrible."

"Lots of guys get into fights," I pointed out.

Marsha rolled her eyes.

"Some of the team members are from other schools," Patrick said. "Maybe they stole it."

I shook my head. "How would they even know we had a new laser printer?"

"Right," agreed Patrick.

"Didn't that curly-haired kid get in trouble last year?" I asked. "Frankie?"

Patrick grinned. "Yeah, he hid the Saint Anthony statue in the furnace room. Then he sent Sister a note. St. Anthony would be returned when pizzas were ordered for the whole seventh grade. If she refused, the fire alarm would be set off."

"That's stupid," said Marsha. "Setting off the

fire alarm is an automatic suspension. Sister warns us about that every year."

"It was just a joke," I said. Bob was nice — he had to be; he was good friends with Strawberry.

"Well," huffed Marsha. "It was a stupid joke. Don't you remember how we all had to stay in for recess that day and help our teacher search our homeroom for Saint Anthony?"

"It was a joke, Marsha." I even added a hearty laugh. "And it was funny, too."

Marsha turned and glared at me. "Yeah, and about as funny as bringing a dead snake to school. Right, Mr. Friday?"

My smile disappeared. Marsha was right. If I had never brought the dead snake to school, Mr. Doyle wouldn't be in any trouble.

If I had kept my sense of humor under lock and key, I wouldn't be dreading my date with Marsha Cessano in the supply closet. But if the plan helped clear Mr. Doyle, I'd be willing to meet Marsha at the altar.

Chapter Fourteen

Patrick promised to go with Marsha when she called her mother about staying after school.

"Oh thanks, Patrick," said Marsha. "And I may have to borrow some money for the call."

"Sure," agreed Patrick. "I always travel with extra money."

"And, Patrick, I hate to be a pest, but could you please, please come with me when I ask Sister about cleaning the copy machine?"

"Patrick will be glad to help you tie your shoes, too, Marsha," I cracked.

They didn't even pretend to look at me. Neither one of them had bothered asking my opinion for the last twenty minutes. Marsha and Patrick were riding on the same wavelength, finishing each other's sentences like an old married couple. The two of them acted like I wasn't even there. And, I was closer to Mr. Doyle than they were — I'd worked off more detentions with him than any other kid in the history of Sacred Heart Elementary school.

"I'm convinced the plan is solid," said Patrick.

I *wasn't* convinced. I was worried. Not only about clearing Mr. Doyle's name, but about Patrick acting like Marsha was his new best friend. In fact, by the time the recess bell rang, my head felt like someone had planted a dozen fondue forks in it. Maybe I had an allergy to Marsha. In fact I was *sure* that I did. Patrick and I could have thought up a plan on our own. Without Miss Takeover Marsha.

During the last period of the day, Mr. Doyle wheeled the projector in for Mrs. Pompalini.

Great, I thought, remembering we were going to watch a film during science. But then I saw how sad Mr. Doyle looked, how hard he was concentrating on setting up the projector and getting the screen to stay down. Mrs. Pompalini thanked him, but he still kept asking if everything was okay. Finally, I just looked down at my desk. It was too painful to watch Mr. Doyle acting so unsure of himself. What if he just quit?

That's when I decided to forget about how I felt about Marsha and join forces with her. The plan had to work, and it had to work fast.

After the dismissal bell rang and buses were called, Patrick, Marsha, and I said good-bye to Mrs. Pompalini and hurried out to our lockers.

"Okay, we'll meet in the gym in about ten or fifteen minutes," said Marsha.

"Better make it fifteen," suggested Patrick. "We want to make sure all the players are there."

"Make it twenty," I said. "Eddie is always late."

Marsha grabbed her jacket and slammed her locker. "Okay. I'll see you guys in twenty. Remember, make sure you notice my bracelet and be loud."

"I know my lines," said Patrick.

"Nobody gave me any lines," I pointed out.

"You don't *need* any lines, Roger," said Marsha. "You might just mess them up anyway."

"No, I won't." I glanced over at Patrick, waiting for him to jump in and defend me. Surely Patrick knows that a kid who can memorize the Pirates' schedule, their starting line-up, *and* their batting averages, could remember a few measly lines.

"Roger, it might be easier if I notice Marsha's bracelet and then *I* tell her she better take it off before she cleans the copy machine." Patrick smiled. "Just to make sure we both aren't repeating the same lines. Marsha and I rehearsed it a few times while you were gone."

Marsha nodded. "Yeah. If you really *have* to say something, Roger, just say, 'Wow!' or something when you see my bracelet."

"Wow!" I mumbled. I should be able to remember that.

"See you!" cried Marsha as she headed down the hall.

Patrick grabbed his bookbag. "Come on, Roger. We don't want to be late."

Mr. Doyle was sitting in his office when we got downstairs. He had three cartons of milk lined up on his desk.

"Come on in, boys," he said. "I got us some milk from the cafeteria."

"Thanks, Mr. Doyle." I reached for mine and sat down on a bundle of newspapers.

"We better save that for later," said Patrick. He

98

set his bookbag down and reached for a scraper. "I think we better get upstairs and get to work."

"Oh," Mr. Doyle said. He set his milk down and looked worried, as if Patrick were telling us all to get busy.

"Well, I'm thirsty," I said, taking another gulp of milk to show Mr. Doyle how much I appreciated it.

"Roger," said Patrick. He tapped his watch.

Mr. Doyle stood up and put his milk on a shelf. "Patrick is right, Roger. Time to get to work."

But I wouldn't get up for a minute or two. I sat on the newspapers, drinking my milk, and joking with Mr. Doyle.

It was hard getting Mr. Doyle to laugh. He tried, but he was thinking about other things. He kept checking his cleaning cart and asking us if we thought he had enough rags. He never asked us about that before.

I was scared. Our plan had to work. And fast!

Chapter Fifteen

"Our first job will be in the principal's office. We need to clean the inside of Sister's windows," suggested Mr. Doyle. "This morning, I noticed they didn't look so nice."

Patrick's face flushed red. "They looked okay to me." He jerked his head toward the gym. "I think we should start in the gym. Like we usually do."

"*Then* we could do Sister's windows," I said cheerfully. I didn't want to start telling Mr. Doyle what to do. After all, he was in charge of us.

"I want to get those windows before Sister locks up. It won't take long," said Mr. Doyle. He wheeled his cart past the gym and headed down the hall. "Come on, boys."

"Now what are we going to do?" hissed Patrick. "Marsha will drop over when we all march in the office."

"Relax," I whispered back. "We'll hurry up with the windows and then head back down to the gym. We told Marsha we would meet her there in twenty minutes."

"Yeah, but you already *wasted* ten minutes, drinking that milk," snapped Patrick. "Didn't you get the message I was trying to send you?"

"Yes, your brilliant lordship, lowly Roger Friday was able to understand your message. I just thought it might be nice to enjoy the milk Mr. Doyle took the trouble to bring us."

"Don't be so sensitive, Roger. The important thing is to clear Mr. Doyle's name. Which means we have to stick to the original plan. Marsha and I agreed that . . ."

I started walking again, trying not to let what Patrick was saying get to me. After all, he had been my best friend since kindergarten. My Marsha-allergies must have been acting up again.

"Hurry up, boys," called Mr. Doyle from the end of the hall.

We didn't see Marsha in the office. Maybe Sister

had sent her down to the cafeteria to run the copy machine through the dishwasher.

The windows didn't take long, especially with Patrick Windexing and wiping so fast I thought his arm was going to unwind from his body.

"Now for the gym," cried Patrick as he headed down the hall. "I'll meet you there."

Mr. Doyle laughed. "That Patrick sure is a worker, Roger."

I hung back, watching Mr. Doyle take his time to turn off every light, and lock the door. He even jiggled the doorknob.

"Mr. Doyle, don't worry about the laser printer," I said as we were walking down the hall to the gym. "The police are really good about catching thieves."

Mr. Doyle nodded. "But, I listen to the radio, Roger. Sometimes they don't catch them. Sometimes they just get away with it."

"Yeah," I agreed. "I know."

Mr. Doyle pulled open the gym door and let me push the cleaning cart in. "But, we hope they catch the thief. Then our school will have a good printer. The kids like to write stories."

"Yeah, the sooner they catch him the better,"

I mumbled. I meant that. Not only would it mean an end to Mr. Doyle's worrying, but it would end the intense detective work with Marsha. She was beginning to cause trouble between Patrick and me.

"Okay, run those suicides!" yelled Coach Evarts. He blasted his whistle and watched as Strawberry and the others raced back and forth across the gym floor.

"They sure are fast," said Mr. Doyle.

We watched them run. Mr. Doyle started telling me about his older brother, Adam, who played college football years ago. He also had a sister who ran a hunting lodge in Connecticut.

I liked hearing about his family. I liked knowing that he had a life outside Sacred Heart Elementary. People who would take care of him in case he got in trouble, or just needed some help.

"Well, hello!"

Marsha stood in the doorway of the gym, her sleeves pushed up, and her voice turned up to High Voltage.

"I've been looking for you, Patrick!" she screamed. She shook back her hair and waved her arm back and forth. She stopped mid-wave to unhook her bracelet from her sleeve. Then she waved some more.

"Hi, Patrick," she shrieked again, walking quickly across the gym, frantically waving her arm back and forth with all the velocity needed to stop a speeding freight train.

Our plan was in motion.

Chapter Sixteen

"Oh, hi, Marsha!" shouted Patrick. He even mumbled something about her bracelet. That's when I ran over to inform him that until the suicides were finished, the players couldn't hear anything but the slapping of basketball shoes back and forth across the gym.

Marsha looked flustered, as if a director had yelled "CUT!!!!" in the middle of her best lines. "They're going to start wondering exactly why I'm here."

I sighed. "First of all, Marsha, I don't think any of them even *know* you are here. And second of all, if you're so worried about it, get to work." I slapped a gum scraper in her hand. "Remember,

Marsha, your job is to get rid of the gum, not to rechew it."

"Ohhhhhhhh, gross!" she shrieked.

Actually, as she was shrieking, a few of the players did look over our way.

"Just scrape a little bit until it quiets down," said Patrick. He was trying hard not to smile at me. But I knew he was weakening. He was also seeing Marsha as her true, big mouth, overreacting self.

After ten more minutes of drills and lay-up work, Coach Evarts blasted his whistle again and told the team to sit down. He wanted to talk to them about the big game.

Marsha dropped her scraper and raced to her spot. The girl may have a big mouth, but she was a professional.

"Oh, Patrick," she hollered. "I've been looking for you."

Patrick looked confused, which made sense since Marsha had been scraping big wads of gum next to him for the past ten minutes.

"Hi, Marsha," Patrick rushed in. "What an expensive bracelet. Don't get ink on it."

I laughed. "You're jumping ahead of your lines, Patrick!"

Marsha glared at me. "Oh, yes," she screamed. "Thank you for reminding me. I better take off this real diamond bracelet before I have to go clean Sister's copy machine!"

"The office is locked," called out Mr. Doyle.

By this time, half the team had turned around, wondering what all the shouting was about. I decided to try for an Oscar myself.

"Yes, the office is locked, but luckily Sister left the copy machine in the hall, Marsha," I cried. "So, why don't you let Patrick and me hold that diamond bracelet for you? After all, things are disappearing around here."

I felt like taking a bow. I had fixed Mr. Doyle's *faux pas*, and slid Marsha into an easy opportunity to hand over the bracelet. I looked up and smiled at Marsha. The girl had to be grateful.

"You idiot," hissed Marsha and Patrick at the same time.

I refrained from bowing. Where was the gratitude?

"Marsha, you better hide the bracelet someplace safe," Patrick ranted. He pointed to the door. "Someplace *safe,* Marsha."

Marsha looked confused. Obviously she wasn't much of an impromptu actress.

"Like your locker," I shouted.

"Be quiet!" hissed Marsha. "That was *my* line."

Marsha shook back her hair and turned slightly, her arm and bracelet extended toward the team. By this time, even Coach Evarts was scratching his head and looking annoyed.

"Yes, I think I shall go directly to my locker and *hide* my bracelet. Yes, good old G 108. My trusty locker. Farewell, I mean, good-bye!"

Marsha walked slowly across to the locker room, her arm still extended, the bracelet still twinkling.

Patrick looked so proud of Marsha, I was afraid he was going to burst into tears. If he had had a rose, he would have tossed it.

"Get busy scraping," I mumbled, scraping my way toward him.

"Wasn't she great?" sighed Patrick.

"Yeah, a real credit to the human race," I agreed. "If we can only find a classification for her, she could have her own exhibit at the museum."

Patrick scowled. "Why are you so hard on her, Roger?"

"Me?" I squeaked. "Patrick, listen to yourself. Aren't you the same guy who helped me pour Jell-O in her boots last year?"

Patrick closed his eyes as if the memory was too painful.

"Oh, brother," I growled. "By the time you really get to know her, Patrick, it will be too late. She will have already sold you that acre in the Florida swamp."

Patrick bent down and started scraping. He glared at me once, and then stabbed his scraper into an especially large wad of purple-passion-grape.

Chapter Seventeen

Twenty minutes later, Patrick and I convinced Mr. Doyle that we needed a five-minute break. I was praying we would only need five minutes to catch the thief, clear Mr. Doyle's name, and return to our gum scraping, at which I was beginning to excel.

Once out in the hall, Patrick rubbed his hands together. "Okay, now comes the tricky part. We have to make sure no one sees us sneaking into the supply closet."

"Piece of cake," I assured him. "The tricky part will be keeping our sanity while being cooped up with Marsha."

Patrick frowned at me. "She came up with the plan, Roger."

"Right," I admitted. And anyone who liked Mr. Doyle couldn't be all bad.

The coast was clear. Patrick and I opened the door to the supply closet. Marsha was already there, sitting on an overturned bucket.

"Hurry up," she whispered from her throne.

We hopped inside and closed the door. It was dark. Very dark. The whole closet was no larger than a four-foot square, filled to capacity with Patrick, Marsha, me, and a trillion buckets and cleaning supplies.

I sniffed some pine cleaner and Marsha's strawberry shampoo. Both made me slightly dizzy.

"I can't see a thing," pointed out Patrick.

"Bend down and look out through the vent, like me," suggested Marsha. "Pull up a bucket."

Patrick and I fumbled around in the dark. A bucket fell and an icy cold liquid filled up my shoe.

"Gross!" I muttered. "Turn on a light."

"Be quiet," hissed the queen. "I hear someone coming. Get down!"

Patrick and I pressed our faces against the vent. A pair of very large, black tennis shoes came closer and closer.

Marsha dove her head into my chest, her fingernails digging into my arm. "I'm scared," she muttered.

"Shhhhhhh," I choked.

The supply closet was quiet for one long moment. A trickle of sweat slid slowly down my spine. The legs were still outside the vent. Waiting, but for what? The diamond bracelet was across the hall in Marsha's locker. Nothing was inside the supply closet but pine cleaner and three scared fifth-graders.

Just then the door opened. The bright light from the hall flooded into the closet. Boing! Patrick, Marsha, and I popped up like a trio of jack-in-the-boxes.

"Yikes!" cried Marsha, tripping over her bucket as she tumbled out into the hall.

I stumbled out, falling against Bob from the basketball team.

"What are you guys doing?"

Marsha stood up, smoothing down her hair. Her face was scarlet. "We, I . . . I was just leaving."

Bob started to laugh. "Whoa, having a little party in the supply closet, huh? I don't think Sister would be too thrilled to hear about this."

Marsha reached out and swatted Bob lightly on

the arm. "Oh, be quiet! We were in the supply closet on business, you, you tall person, you!"

Patrick and I stepped out of the closet, trying to look as cool as possible. Managers of the Best of the Block team didn't need any bad publicity.

"Isn't this cute," Bob said. "What were you three doing in there?"

"None of your business," snapped Marsha. She shook back her hair. "Now, if you will excuse me, I have to go."

Patrick took a few steps after Marsha. "Yeah, and maybe I should go, too."

Bob nodded. "Good idea. Maybe I should go down to have a talk with Sister. I don't think she likes romantic meetings on school grounds."

"Oh, be quiet," snapped Marsha. "If you say one word to Sister about this, I'll . . ."

Bob smiled. "You'll what?"

Marsha's face grew pinker, her lower lip starting to tremble. "Just don't say anything, okay?"

"Of course not. What do you think I am — a snitch?"

Patrick and Marsha flew down the hall. I stayed.

"So, what are you doing out here?" I finally asked.

Bob looked surprised. "Who wants to know?"

I shrugged. "I just wondered what you needed in the supply closet."

Bob rolled his eyes. "Supplies, what else?" He grabbed a bottle of cleaner. "Seems your friend the janitor missed a few spots."

Bob tried to slam the door, but not before I noticed the box that Patrick and I had been sitting on.

"So what are you waiting for?" asked Bob. "Think your girlfriend is coming back? What are you, in the fifth grade?"

I shivered. "She isn't my girlfriend."

Bob snorted. "She sure has a temper."

I smiled. "Yeah. Well, I guess I better be getting back."

Bob started to walk with me. "You're the kid Strawberry was talking about, right? You and your friend are going to help with the tournament."

I nodded. "If we don't end up with any more detention. I seem to specialize in it."

Bob nudged me with his elbow. "Stay on Sister's good side," he snickered. "If you can find it." He pulled open the gym door. "*After* you."

As I started to walk in, Bob handed me the bottle

of cleaner. "Do me a favor, okay? Put this over on the bench. I need to get a quick drink before the Coach sees me."

I nodded, gripping the cleaner. But as soon as the gym doors closed, I raced down the gym and grabbed Patrick. His face was still beet red.

"Pat, come on. I need a witness." I set the cleaner down and started toward the door.

Patrick caught up. "What are you talking about? Let's just stay here. Marsha's afraid Bob is going to get us all in trouble."

"I saw something in the supply closet. Hurry!" I muttered.

We walked quietly down the empty hall. As we rounded the bend, I pushed Patrick and shoved him into the alcove of the girls' restroom.

Patrick glanced up at the sign and yelped. "What are we doing here? Are you trying to get us kicked out of school?"

"Shhhhhhh," I clamped my hand over his mouth and pointed toward the supply closet.

"What is he doing?" Patrick whispered.

Bob was opening the supply closet door and stepping inside.

115

Chapter Eighteen

I had to drag Patrick down the hall.

"We shouldn't be doing this," he muttered.

"Trust me."

When we were outside the closet, I yanked the door open.

Bob blinked in the light, his arms wrapped around a box.

"Gotcha!" I said.

"You don't got a thing. Now move and forget you ever saw me."

"It's the laser printer. What are you doing with it?"

Bob beamed. "I found it in the supply closet."

Patrick grinned. "Well, that's great." He

glanced at me. "Isn't that great, Rog?"

I shrugged. "I guess it's great if you just happened to find the printer. But, it's not so great if you were the one who put the printer in the supply closet in the first place."

"Well, tonight I am borrowing this printer, and tomorrow I'll put it back in the supply closet. I'm not stealing it."

"You took it yesterday, didn't you?" I asked.

"Be quiet," said Bob. "Your word against mine. You two were in the supply closet before I got there. Who's to say you didn't steal it?"

"Put the printer back," I suggested. "I'll tell Sister it's back."

"I *need* this printer. I'm *not* stealing it, either. I jammed ours the other day and my brother is ready to kill me. He has two papers locked inside the computer and if I don't bring this home tonight, I won't have an arm left to play with."

"People are blaming Mr. Doyle," I pointed out.

"No one would believe he took it," Bob said. "When the printer shows up tomorrow, all this will be yesterday's news. I only need the printer for one night. Don't say anything."

"You can't just take it," I said.

Bob headed down toward the entrance. "Just keep quiet about this. I'm going to slide this outside and come back for it later. No one has to know."

"We already know," Patrick said.

"Yeah," said Bob. "Lucky for me you two are good sports and won't tell on me."

"Please, don't take it, Bob," I said. "This isn't funny."

Bob laughed. "Listen to who's talking. Aren't you the kid who brings dead snakes to school?"

"I don't get other people in trouble," I answered.

Bob started walking. "I'm only borrowing it. Give me a break."

Patrick elbowed me. "Let's get going."

"Come on, Bob. You know you shouldn't do this."

"Who's going stop me?"

"Me." My voice was a bleat.

"You and who else?" Bob laughed.

"Me and . . ." I glanced around the hall. Patrick flattened himself against the lockers, shaking his head. I reached for the fire alarm.

"Bob, all I have to do is flip the switch and

someone will be here." Fire alarms were a big deal at Sacred Heart.

"Automatic suspension for you if you hit the alarm," Bob reminded me. "And Sister might just forget to let you back in."

I nodded, trying to smile. "I might just end up living with Gramma Olenski."

"Look, relax. Nobody's going to get in trouble," Bob said.

"I'm going to pull this unless you set the printer down," I said.

"Go on, Friday," he said. "I *dare* you!"

It's dangerous to dare a funny guy.

I hit the alarm!

Chapter Nineteen

Within seconds the hall was filled with people. The weird part was, nobody was screaming and running around in circles like they do in the movies. Coach Evarts raced out with his clipboard, followed by his team. Mr. Doyle hurried out and grabbed the fire extinguisher from the wall, and Sister Mary Elizabeth charged up the hall with a worried expression on her face. Everyone was doing a job.

"What is going on?" Sister Mary Elizabeth asked Coach Evarts. "Is there a fire?"

As soon as Sister spoke, Bob turned around, set the box down, and stood in front of it like he was waiting for a bus.

Coach shrugged and started asking his players if they smelled smoke.

"No fire, Sister!" I said. "Sorry. I set off the fire alarm."

Mr. Doyle ran up to Sister, his key chain bobbing up and down on his belt. "You want me to go turn off the alarm, Sister? I got my key right here."

Sister nodded. "Yes. The office is open. Call the fire department, Mr. Doyle. Tell them it was a false alarm." Sister turned and scowled at me then. "All right, Roger. Suppose you tell me what happened."

Coach Evarts ordered his team back into the gym.

I glanced over at Bob.

"Answer me, Roger," continued Sister. "You've gotten into a lot of trouble lately, but this takes the cake. Have you any idea of the seriousness of your latest prank?"

"It wasn't a prank, Sister."

Sister groaned. "Prank, joke, what's the difference?"

I shook my head. "No. It wasn't a joke. I pulled it on purpose."

"On purpose?" Sister's voice rose an octave.

"Yes, Sister. I'm sorry."

Sister looked down the hall then, focusing in on Bob. "Bob, shouldn't you be in the gym practicing with the Coach?"

Bob nodded. "Yes, Sister."

"Well, go inside then," Sister said, dismissing him with a wave of her hand.

"Roger, come with me," said Sister. "We'll talk about this down in my office."

"Will I really get thrown out of school?"

The alarm stopped.

"Thank goodness," Sister sighed. "I don't know what gets into you, Roger."

"Maybe I'll be thrown out of the altar boys," I added. "In fact, I shouldn't be allowed to ride the bus for the rest of the year. I have a used pair of roller skates."

Sister stopped, throwing up both hands. "Roger Friday, have you no shame? You threw the fire alarm, upsetting quite a few people, and now you're rattling on and on about nothing."

Bob picked up the printer and walked quickly toward Sister and me. "Don't be too hard on Roger. He only set the alarm off because he was excited about finding the printer." Bob set the box down in front of Sister. "Look, good as new."

Sister broke into a huge smile. "Roger, you found the printer?"

"He and that big-mouthed girl did," Bob said.

I looked at Bob.

"Now, Roger, you didn't hide the printer as a joke, did you? You've been the biggest trouble-maker in Sacred Heart's history," Sister started. "You've put soap in the punch bowl in kinder-garten, colored on the statue of St. Anthony in first grade . . ."

"A small moustache," I whispered. "An erasable moustache."

"And," continued Sister, "carted in a dead snake just a few days ago. I'm very disappointed in you."

"I'm sorry, Sister." And I was. About everything.

Sister sighed. "You've gone too far this time, Roger. After school detention with Mr. Doyle won't right the wrong, you're suspended for three days."

"Sister, I messed up here," whispered Bob. "It wasn't Roger. He didn't take the printer." Bob stood in front of us, chewing his lip and look-ing a little sick. "Can I talk to you, Sister Mary

Elizabeth?" he asked slowly. He reached into his pocket and handed Sister a key. A small silver key labeled C. "Sorry, Sister."

"Wait for me in my ofice," said Sister. "Call your parents if you want. I'll be down in a few minutes." Sister and I watched Bob carry the printer down the hall. He was moving down the hall as if he had a ton of cement in each tennis shoe. I had made the long walk to Sister's office often enough to know how he felt.

"He was only going to borrow it," I said.

"Borrowers ask, Roger. I'll get Bob's side of the story in a few minutes. Roger," said Sister. "I have three points of business to clear up with you."

"Yes, Sister," I said. In trouble again.

Sister handed me a key. "First, I thought you might like to be the one to return this key to Mr. Doyle. It belongs on his key ring."

"Thanks, Sister." I took the key and turned it around and around in my hand. "You have no idea how happy Mr. Doyle will be to have this back."

"Yes, I do." Sister sighed. "I didn't want to have to take his key away. But I'm the principal. I have to keep lots of people happy. I knew Mr. Doyle was having a hard time. I've known him a long, long time."

"I've known him since kindergarten," I said.

Sister nodded. "When I was in eighth grade at Sacred Heart, Mr. Doyle was in the second grade," said Sister. "I didn't know him very well, but I heard about his accident. It happened right before school. Every classroom went to church that day to pray for him."

"You . . . you were a kid here?" I asked.

Sister rolled her eyes. "Did you really think they ordered me from a nun magazine, Roger?"

I cracked up. "Sorry."

"So, I do have a special place in my heart for Mr. Doyle." Sister took off her glasses and rubbed her eyes. "Just like you do, Roger."

I felt funny all of a sudden, like part of me wanted to cry and part of me wanted to shout for joy.

"So," Sister finally said. "This brings me to the second point of business, Mr. Friday."

"Oh, no," I groaned. "Sister, you don't have to call my mom, do you? She's had kind of a rough week."

"Haven't we all," laughed Sister. "Actually, I wanted to know if you could follow up on a few phone calls for me, Roger. Coach Evarts mentioned your new program idea. It seems that I have four or five friends who own businesses in the area, and I think they would love to buy a big ad for our Best of the Block program."

"Great!" I was so excited, I almost hugged Sister. But since I've never hugged her before, I settled for another "Great! If we sell enough ads, maybe Gym Rat, I mean Jim Rattner, could ask his uncle to help us to get new jerseys for the team. I mean, if they still want them."

"New jerseys would be great. We could use the old ones for practice. The Best of the Block will certainly appreciate Jim's help." Sister checked her watch. "Well, I better go down and talk to Bob. Please don't talk about the printer situation to anyone, Roger."

I shook my head. "I never liked publicity myself, Sister."

"Good," agreed Sister. "Now for the third and final point of business, Roger."

"Ready when you are, Sister," I said. Having

a business meeting with Sister Mary Elizabeth was fun. Downright enjoyable. We worked well together.

"It has always been Sacred Heart's policy to regard the fire alarm as an important link to the fire department, Roger." Sister cleared her throat and frowned. "Which is why the punishment for pulling the fire alarm without reason has always been an automatic suspension."

I gulped. "But, Sister, I had a reason. Patrick, Marsha, and I were trying to clear Mr. Doyle's name. We set up a trap, but when that didn't work, I had to freelance. Wing it. Use the old thinking machine."

"Patrick and Marsha helped you with your planing?" asked Sister.

"Yes," I said quickly. Sister loved Patrick Frank. She would probably shake my hand for asking such a brilliant kid to assist me. And Marsha Cessano had just cleaned Sister's copy machine. That ought to buy a few points.

"This changes everything," Sister said slowly.

It was hard not to give Sister a high-five. Things were going so well.

"Since the three of you were involved," began Sister, "I think the punishment should be amended."

I shrugged. "Sure." If Sister wanted to forget the whole thing, that was fine with me.

Sister stood up straighter and put her hand on my shoulder. "In light of this new information, Roger, you will not be suspended for pulling the fire alarm."

I tried to look surprised. "Great. Thanks, Sister."

"You better save your thanks, Roger."

Chapter Twenty

After Sister had a long talk with Bob about the stolen printer, she had a short talk with Patrick, Marsha, and me. She didn't call our parents; she felt we could all work this out together. She flipped through the Sacred Heart rule book to make sure we hadn't broken a few. We had. There was a 1964 rule against students' hiding in lockers or closets and one against pulling fire alarms. Instead of kicking us out of school, Sister suggested that the three of us *volunteer* to help out at the annual retired nuns' card party at the convent. It would only take two hours of washing dishes, passing dip and chips, and generally trying to look cheerful and innocent.

129

So, here we were, the three of us, standing outside the dark brown bricks of the convent on a sunny Saturday afternoon.

"I can't believe Sister is so ungrateful!" groaned Marsha as soon as my dad's car pulled away. "After all, we *did* solve the case of the stolen printer. Why isn't the school dedicating a stained glass window to us, instead of making us serve punch and cookies to a bunch of old nuns?"

Patrick and I laughed. My mother had actually hugged me and cried when I told her I wanted to volunteer my time. She said I was such a nice boy.

"It's kind of funny, really," said Patrick. "My dad said his first-grade teacher will probably be here. Sister Celeste."

Marsha shook back her hair and started up the steps to the front door. "Yeah? Well, I see nothing funny about it."

"It's better than Bob's Saturday, Marsha," I pointed out. "I heard he got suspended for three days *and* kicked off the Best of the Block. He won't be wearing those great new jerseys our program ads paid for. Gym Rat's uncle got us a great deal!"

"At least Sister didn't press charges. Bob must feel terrible," Patrick said.

"But he was *guilty* about something," insisted Marsha. "Why am I being forced to be a maid in the convent?"

"Need I mention that you broke the 1964 rule against hiding in closets?" I reminded. "Although Sister didn't seem too mad. Hey, Marsha, maybe Sister's trying to recruit you. Marsha, a nun on the run."

"Do me a favor and go run out and play in traffic, Roger," snapped Marsha. "Do you know how hard it was trying to convince my mother that I wanted to do this? I think she was a little worried about me. She kept asking me if I felt all right."

I elbowed her. "You are a little green. But I think that's your normal color, isn't it?"

Marsha elbowed me back and tried to walk faster.

"Marsha, it's not that bad," said Patrick. "Sister could have called our parents and made a big deal about the three of us playing hide-and-seek in the supply closet."

Marsha spun around and glared at Patrick.

"Don't ask me why I ever thought you were smart, Patrick. You are just as dumb as your friend, Roger."

Patrick and I laughed harder than ever. I felt great. Not overjoyed at the thought of passing cheese and crackers to a group of retired nuns, but great knowing that Mr. Doyle had his computer room key back, Marsha was in her usual rotten mood, and Patrick and I were best buddies again.

"Just stay far away from me, you two." Marsha rang the bell on the heavy wooden door.

The door swung open and a short nun with white hair smiled at the three of us. "Hello there, children. Come in."

We walked in and stopped in the middle of a large entry. The room was pretty, with lots of light coming in from the windows and a huge basket of flowers on the center table.

"I'm Sister Celeste!" she said cheerfully. "I'm eighty-seven years old today."

"Sister Celeste?" asked Patrick. He stuck out his hand. "Hello, Sister. I'm Patrick Frank. You taught my dad first grade."

Sister nodded. "I'll bet I did."

"Ron Frank," added Patrick. "Maybe you called him Ronnie."

Sister's cheeks grew redder. Her smile froze for a second. "I'm afraid some days I don't remember as well as other days. Like this morning, I was making a dip for crackers, and I kept thinking, 'Now, did I add those black beans, already, and did I forget the pepper.' " Sister reached for Marsha's coat and smiled. "You'll have to be sure and try my dip, children."

Sister Mary Elizabeth hurried in and dragged us all to the kitchen.

"Now, everyone will be here soon. Marsha, turn the kettle on, please, and make sure you keep stirring the pudding." Sister handed us each an apron. "Patrick, you will be in charge of collecting coats, and Roger, I want you to take orders for tea or soft drinks."

"When will the pudding be done?" asked Marsha.

Sister glanced into the pot. "Five minutes. Keep stirring and then just . . ."

The front bell was ringing. Sister took Patrick

133

and me by the arms and steered us back out into the hall. "Okay, children, now remember your manners. Be pleasant."

I turned around and grinned at Marsha, alone with kitchen detail. She stuck out her tongue at me.

Sister knew her helpers, all right. She was a smart lady to hide Marsha in the kitchen.

Within ten minutes, the whole convent was filled with nuns. Most of them were a lot older than the nuns teaching at the school. Two of them had to be pushed to their card tables in their wheelchairs. Patrick had a head start and his nun beat me to the table, but at least my nun didn't scream as we rounded the bend.

Sister gave me a little notepad to collect drink orders. It was fun. I drew a little picture of each nun and then printed what she wanted beside it.

I figured I could only handle five orders at a time, so I raced back into the kitchen. I passed Patrick who was struggling up the stairs with his arms filled with black coats. How did nuns tell them apart?

I was thinking that maybe we should stick a piece of paper with the nun's name in her coat pocket, as I pushed open the kitchen door.

The room was filled with light gray smoke, a terrible scorched smell as if someone had been trying to cook a camel, and a maniac named Marsha running around in circles, saying "Oh, my gosh. Oh, my gosh!"

I slipped inside and tried my best to calm her down.

"Hello, honey," I said. "I'm home!"

Chapter Twenty-one

Marsha flew into my arms. Actually, she rushed to me and tried to strangle me.

"You've got to help me," she sobbed, shaking me by the shoulders. "I only took my eyes off the pudding for a second, and the next thing I knew it . . . it exploded. I ruined it. Sister is going to kill me."

I pried her off me and hurried over to the stove. I turned off the flame under the pudding pot and then turned on the exhaust fan. The contents of the pudding pan did not look like pudding.

Marsha glanced nervously at the door. "What am I going to tell Sister? I think this pudding was supposed to be the frosting for Sister Celeste's birthday cake. Sister said she can't eat too much sugar and this was some special pudding and . . ." Marsha paused long enough to burst into tears. She was mumbling behind her hands.

I pulled her hands down. "What?"

"I said, poor Sister Celeste. It's her birthday and I ruined her pudding. I never do anything right."

My mouth fell open.

"And I ruined Sister's pan," continued Marsha, wiping under each eye with her apron.

"Hey, don't give up the ship," I said. "I burned up a macaroni pan last week."

Marsha looked hopeful. "What did you do?"

"Threw the pan away. It was a mess. That macaroni was cemented to the bottom."

"Great," muttered Marsha, taking a pot holder and carrying the pan to the sink. She got a spoon and started throwing the blackened pudding down the garbage disposal. "I just know Sister will find some 1976 rule that says anyone who tries to burn convent property gets kicked out of school."

"Here," I said, grabbing the pan. "Fill this list of drinks and set it on the tray. I don't want Sister coming in here till I think of a plan."

Marsha shuddered. "I never want to hear the word 'plan' again. Plans are ruining my life."

She got the drinks and set them on the tray. "Here, Roger."

I was busy scraping some of the bigger black chunks off with a butter knife. The pan was clattering around in the sink like it was trying to escape.

"You take it out, Marsha. This pan is trying to make a run for it."

Marsha wiped her face with a dish towel and sighed. "Thanks for helping me, Roger. I'm sorry I said you were a jerk."

"You said I was dumb," I muttered as I rinsed the pan. "Not a jerk."

"I said both. I called you a jerk about twenty times as I was stirring the pudding." Marsha picked up the tray. "Well, here goes nothing. Maybe I should just keep walking. Or maybe I *should* become a nun. I don't think nuns are allowed to yell at each other."

I grabbed a bottle of liquid soap and attacked the pan. "Don't worry. I think I'm making progress."

"But what about the pudding? Sister said everyone was going to sing to Sister Celeste at the end of the card party." Marsha's eyes started to fill up again. "Roger, Sister Celeste is eighty-seven years old. I mean, it's not like she has another twenty birthdays to look forward to."

Marsha had a point there. I glanced at the two-layer cake on the counter. It did look a little bare.

"Marsha, take the drinks out. Take a few more orders and write them on my pad, and then run outside and pick a few flowers."

"What?"

"Just a few. Five or six. We can throw them on top of the cake and it will look great. My mom decorates with parsley and flowers a lot. Besides, flowers are very low in sugar."

Marsha almost smiled. "Yeah, and we can put green leaves around the bottom. Sister won't be so mad if the cake looks great."

"Hurry up, though," I warned. "I don't want Sister coming in to see what's holding up the drinks."

Marsha turned around and started to back out of the door, carefully balancing the tray and drinks. "But, Roger, what are we going to do about the pan?"

I rinsed the pan again, staring at its bottom as millions of tiny soap bubbles rose up from the sink. The pan looked a little better, but mostly it looked like a burned-up pan.

"Maybe I should call my mom," I suggested. "Sometimes our good silverware and silver trays turn black. My mom has this special, stinky gray goop that she spreads all over it and it really works."

"My mom has that, too!" cried Marsha.

I shook off my hands and looked under the sink. It wasn't there.

Marsha groaned and backed out of the kitchen. I picked up my knife and went back to work. My right arm was just about to fall off, when I spotted the bowl of goop, right next to the sink.

I reached into the cool goop, grabbing a hefty handful and smearing it around and around the burned bottom of the pan.

"Come on, baby, do your stuff!" I cried. I could feel bits and pieces of the burned pudding lifting free from the bottom.

"Yes, sireeee!" I cried, reaching for another glob. This stuff was magic. This stuff was better than my mother's own polish. Maybe Sister would let me take a baggie home for my mom. Who would have thought I would learn something new in a convent?

I was almost at the bottom of the bowl, practically finished with the pan, when Sister Mary Elizabeth walked in.

"What's burning?" asked Sister.

I held up the pan. "Just a little pudding, but it's all clean now."

Marsha rushed in behind Sister, holding a fistful of flowers. "Ooops, sorry, Sister. I burned the pudding."

"The pan's fine," I said, holding it up for inspection. "Your polish is great, Sister. Worked like magic."

"Oh, great," said Marsha. She rushed over and looked at the pan.

I held up the bowl of gray polish. "Can I take some home to my mom? We have some real dirty trays to clean."

Sister had been frowning, even staring at the kitchen and shaking her head. But when she saw me holding the polish, she actually sank into a chair.

"Oh, no!" she cried.

"I . . . I didn't use it all," I said quickly.

"We'll buy you some more," added Marsha.

Sister groaned and leaned her chin in her hand. "Oh, what am I going to do now?"

Marsha and I hurried over to the table. How expensive could pan polish be?

"I'm really sorry, Sister," I stammered. "I hope this stuff didn't come from Rome."

Sister glanced up at both of us. She bit her lip, and then covered her face with her hands. Within seconds, her shoulders were shaking up and down.

I felt terrible. Never, in all my years as a trouble-maker at Sacred Heart, had I ever made a nun *cry!*

"Sister," I pleaded. "I'm sorry about the polish. I was just trying to teach Marsha everything I know about cleaning pans."

That's when Sister uncovered her face and I could see the tears streaming down her cheeks. She wiped them away with her fingertips and started laughing.

"Roger, promise me you will never teach anyone everything you know. I can only take one of you."

142

"She's laughing!" cried Marsha.

Sister reached out for the glop and smiled at it. "I really don't know how to thank you, children. You saved me."

"From what?" I asked.

Sister glanced down at the pan polish and grinned. "From Sister Celeste's awful dip!"

Patrick came rushing into the kitchen. "Hey, what's burning?"

"The pudding," Marsha and I answered.

Once Sister started laughing again, Marsha and I joined in.

"What's so funny?" Patrick wanted to know. "A zillion nuns asked me for more tea and a few more wanted me to check to see if the convent is on fire."

Marsha smiled. "Things are fine, now, Patrick."

"Never better," I agreed. "No need to pull the fire alarm."

"Fine for you two, maybe," grumbled Patrick. "But, I'm exhausted. And the birthday nun, Sister Celeste, wants to know where her dip is."

Sister started smiling, then laughing again. Marsha and I both started to howl.

"So what should I tell her?" asked Patrick. You

could see how mad he was getting. "What should I say?"

Sister stopped smiling, looking up at me.

"Well," I said, glancing down at the empty bowl, "tell her the truth, Patrick."

Patrick let out a long sigh. "Which is?"

"That I polished it off."

Sister got up from her chair, still smiling. She took the dip bowl to the sink. I wasn't sure what she was going to say when she turned around. Would she remember she was the principal and slap on another detention? Maybe helping out at the Sunday bingo at the church hall.

But when Sister turned around, she was still smiling.

"I'll handle the rest, children. You can get your coats and call your parents about a ride. Thanks for helping."

"Are you sure?" I asked.

"Yes." Sister reached on top of a shelf and handed us each an envelope. "If I ever hear Sister Celeste is bringing her bean dip again, I might ask you three to please come and help me."

"Anytime," we agreed.

While we were waiting for Patrick's mom to pick

144

us up, we opened our envelopes. Inside each was a holy card and five dollars.

I'll always remember that Saturday, and not just because Marsha almost burned down the convent, or because I got paid for serving a detention.

It was probably my best time at Sacred Heart. Mr. Doyle's name had been cleared, the Best of the Block had cool jerseys and a great program, but best of all, I had made Sister Mary Elizabeth laugh.

On that Saturday, I played to my toughest crowd: Sister Mary Elizabeth. I made her laugh. I didn't even have to use a dead snake or an insult to do it. All I did was be me, Roger Friday, live from the fifth grade!

About the Author

Colleen O'Shaughnessy McKenna began writing as a child, when she sent off a script for the *Bonanza* series. Ms. McKenna is best known for her Murphy books, the inspiration for which comes from her own family.

This is Ms. McKenna's twelfth book for Scholastic Hardcover.

In addition to the eight books in the Murphy series, Ms. McKenna has written *Merry Christmas, Miss McConnell!*, the young adult novel *The Brightest Light*, and *Good Grief . . . Third Grade*, a spin-off of the Murphy series.

A former elementary school teacher, Ms. McKenna lives in Pittsburgh, Pennsylvania, with her husband and four children.